Daughter of the King

A Novella

God
Bless!

Proverbs 31

Amanda G.
Williams

Daughter of the King

A Novella

Amanda H. Williams

Papa's Girl Publishing, LLC

Papa's Girl Publishing,, LLC
Papa's Girl Publishing is committed to excellence in the publishing industry. The company is based on the message from Philippians 3:12-14.

Daughter of the King

Cover Design by: Mike Smitley
Edited by: Bonnie Verlander
ISBN: 978-0-615-21226-5
Published in the United States of America

Dedicated to the youth of Deermeadows Baptist Church
who served as my inspiration.
God Bless You in all you do!

Chapter 1

"Alexandra! Come here, darlin'."

The rich bass of William King's voice bellowed through the spacious Tudor house that Lexy King had only known as home. She smiled, always somewhat amused at her father's insistent use of her full first name. *No one* called her Alexandra. Not her mother, brothers, friends….no one. No one except William Foster King III---otherwise know to her as Daddy.

"Coming, Daddy!"

Lexy adored her father, and vice versa. Her mother was her mentor, friend, and confidant, but Daddy, well her daddy was who she looked to for approval. Granted, they had their disagreements. In fact, they both possessed the same hard head, but nothing had ever come between them that couldn't be solved with a trip to Cold Stone Creamery. It was pitiful, but she was a sucker for anything with chocolate.

Lexy finished adjusting her ipod and checked the time as she bounded down the stairs. She had just enough time to go for a run before taking a shower and getting ready for an outing to a nearby Starbucks with some friends. As much as she relished her talks with her father, she hoped this one was quick. Her mother's smile greeted her at the bottom of the stairs.

"Slow down, sweetie. There is no need to rush."

Her mother never, ever wanted Lexy to rush. Elizabeth King considered hurriedness a cause of carelessness, and carelessness caused accidents, which was completely unacceptable, especially for her baby girl. "I know Mama. I've got time, but do you know what Daddy wants?" Her mother smiled, like she knew a secret. She cocked an eyebrow and took on the expression of a precocious six year old that spoke 'I'll never tell' in sing song. Lexy rolled her eyes at her parents' alliance. William and Elizabeth King had been married 30 years and the most famous magician would be hard pressed to squeak a single card between them. They were the definition of a united front, one she had grown to appreciate since she became an adult. But sometimes she wished one of them would tell on the other—just once. She shot her mother a playful smile. Lexy's dark wavy pony tail swished around, looking for her father's face. "So...where is he?"

Elizabeth bobbed her head towards the study and moved into the kitchen humming a tune from her favorite gospel group, Signature Sound. Lexy turned around and very nearly skipped through the den into her father's office. "Daddy?"

William King, known to most as William; only her mother called him Will, spun around in his leather chair and grinned from ear to ear. Suddenly, as if on cue, her pet butterflies that resided in her gut, began to dance. She knew *that look*. That look represented her father's idea of encouraging Lexy to come out of her comfort zone and into some unknown activity that would supposedly inspire growth. These opportunities, as her father called them, took on many different faces during her childhood: ballet, piano, violin, every type of sport, student body president….the list went on. It wasn't that Lexy didn't appreciate or even enjoy the activities (for the exception of violin); it was just that the 'push' that began with the not so subtle 'look' was *always* initially painful. "Let's talk, Alexandra."

Lexy plopped in the sleek, mahogany leather chair that sat across from her father's massive cherry wood desk. Inwardly, she coached herself. *Calm down, Lexy. You are an adult. You don't have to do anything you don't want to do.* She bent down to tighten her shoe laces, while looking up at her father. "What's up?"

He came around the desk and handed her a piece of paper. "Read it and tell me what you think."

Lexy sat up, sighed and took the letter from her father, now very curious about its contents. The greeting was addressed to her father, but apparently in regards to her. She scanned the piece of paper and then looked up at her father, confused.

"What is this, Daddy?"

He sat down behind his desk and looked up over the teepee he had constructed with his fingertips.

"Did you read it?"

She nodded slowly and scanned the letter again. "Yes. But it doesn't make sense. I have not heard of Camp Courage and I have no idea who Dr. Joline Darcy is."

Her father explained with a little too much enthusiasm. "Dr. Darcy is actually a good friend of mine. Really, her brother and I were good friends in college. Joline is a bit older…" He shook his head, seemingly shaking off irrelevant thoughts. "Anyway, Joline is the assistant superintendent of schools in a large county up in Georgia."

Lexy continued to stare. "And?"

He chuckled, apparently amused at Lexy's confusion. She, on the other hand, was not. William sobered his laughter. "I talked to

4

her a few months ago. She inherited the responsibility of taking over a summer day camp, Camp Courage. Joline wasn't happy about it; one more thing piled up on dozens of other responsibilities. She was really at a loss as to what to do..."

Lexy, though sometimes accused of being a little feisty, had always been a pretty patient person, especially with her beloved Daddy. Because of her love for her father, Lexy probably only interrupted her father a total of two times in her entire life. Once when he questioned her innocent first date about the validity of his driver's license; another time when he dared approach the subject of puberty when she was 13 years old. But it seemed now warranted an interruption, because nothing coming out of his mouth was making sense. "Daddy…"

He held up his hand to silence her. It worked. She sat back in the chair, noted the ticking time on her watch, and waited. Her jog may be vetoed today.

"Camp Courage is a camp for kids with special needs."

Uh-Oh. Connection. Her degree was in special education. Suddenly, the muddled picture was clearing up. But he wouldn't have volunteered….without even checking….she looked at his face resembling the cat that ate the canary and had just been busted. "Daddy!"

She jumped up from the chair and began pacing. There was a time during her teenage years where she had memorized the number of steps it took to cross from one side of the enormous room to another. It didn't help that her father actually had the gall to appear shocked that she wasn't jumping up and down with excitement. Then, to top it all off, his voice took on the patronizing tone of a parent talking to a child on the brink of a toddler meltdown. "Calm down, sweetheart. It's just an opportunity to think about…"

She rolled her eyes. *Opportunity to think about. Yeah, right. Just like violin, student body president, dance! Really!* Well, not this time. She was twenty two years old and had plans of her own. She was supposed to start graduate school this summer and had actually volunteered to teach summer school. What about her longtime boyfriend, Brody? Apparently, her father hadn't considered any of those factors, or …maybe he had.

He was explaining, "Alexandra, Joline--" He stammered and cleared his throat. "I mean Dr. Darcy needs a qualified someone to direct the day camp for six weeks. It's up in the Augusta area, which is a beautiful city, by the way. You could live with Joline and get lots of invaluable administrative experience. The camp is for children who can't attend any other camps because of their disabilities." He paused a second to let his words sink in. "It would look outstanding on a resume."

Oh, he was pulling out all the stops on this one. She stopped moving and stood in front of him with her arms crossed. He watched her like she was on the verge of some type of conniption. Well this time, he just might be right. Lexy swallowed her aggravation; tried to calm her hyperactive heartbeat, after all, no one could force her to go. It was her decision. She took a deep, cleansing breath and counted to ten. "Daddy, it does sound like a good opportunity. I agree. But it is six hours away. My life is here, in Jacksonville, with you, mom, my friends and Brody."

He actually rolled his eyes. *Aha!* Now this was starting to make sense.

As if he could read her thoughts, he was quick to respond. "Now, wait a minute young lady. Sit down." She did. "I know what you are thinking. And you know as well as I do that is not how I operate." He ran his fingers through his salt and pepper hair, and moved in front of her leaning back on his desk. Lexy always thought her father was handsome with his tall stature and sophisticated presence. But he could also be imposing, and she hated when she was on the receiving end of his sentencing expression. "Alexandra, you have always been a very good girl. You are the light of mine and your mother's life. But you are 22 years old and have never really been out on your own. Jacksonville University is a wonderful school, but its 5 minutes from the home you grew up in. I just think its time you spread your wings a little bit. I'm not against you working at one of the local schools if that is what you choose to do…" He paused as if he was examining the truth of his next statement. "..and I have nothing against Brody."

Lexy leveled him with her hazel eyes.

"Ok, well other than the fact I think you are too young to be so serious about someone." He stopped her upcoming rebuttal. "Not that you are serious about him, but I'm not stupid. He has other intentions, my dear. Honorable, I am sure. But what Brody is thinking is forever. I'm not sure you are ready for that."

Lexy got up from her chair. She had heard enough. "Daddy, you and I both know I'm pretty level headed. Don't you think you can trust me with my own heart…… and career?" She handed the letter back to him and straightened her shoulders, holding her head

8

high, like only he had taught her to do. "Thank you for the opportunity. I will think about it, Daddy. But no promises."

William's eyes filled with pride and then softened towards his grown up girl. He nodded his head, recognizing the end of the discussion. "Understood."

Lexy decided, regardless of the time, to take her jog. She needed time to think and pray. Finding comfort in the sights and sounds of her familiar path, her body began to relax. The sight of the St. Johns River peaking through the giant moss laden oak trees was a source of peace she only found at home. Leave it to her father to turn her well laid out plans upside down. It wasn't that the camp didn't sound like a great experience; it did. But it also scared her, beyond anything she would ever admit to anyone. Her father was right; she hadn't been away from home for any length of time.

Truthfully, she had never desired to leave. Lexy thought about what her parents had written in the pink baby book she often got down from her treasure box just to look through. The penned words were beyond sweet, stating their love for their little girl, but also saying that not one day passed when they didn't pray she would fall in love with Jesus. Their prayers worked because at the early age of 7 she asked Jesus into her heart; it was natural for her, she had loved Him for so long. That love was nurtured in her protective environment. She had two older brothers who were strong Christians, and then there were her parents who set an example of a faith walked out in the daily routine of life. Lexy was one who had been given a childhood where morning devotionals and prayer time were as natural as sitting down to a meal. She attended a private Christian school from Kindergarten through twelfth grade. Her small class was a family, albeit one that fought sometimes, but more like brothers and sisters than anything else. She was never anxious to date, never felt like she was being pulled toward any particular boy. When the time came to choose a college, she never even considered going away from home. Sure, her junior and senior year she moved out and got a small apartment near the private university, but the security of home was only minutes away. Upon graduation, she moved back home and intended to work as a substitute in several different settings before applying for a teaching position the next year. Working on her master's degree seemed like a natural next step, even though she hadn't really consulted God about that move. But she was pretty sure it made sense to get that little insurance policy, in case the classroom wasn't where she wanted to be.

And then, of course there was Brody. She and Brody had met at a Campus Crusade for Christ meeting her sophomore year in college. Brody was a football player and pre-law major. She teased him because he couldn't look more like a preppy golden boy if he tried, which he didn't. He was just wired that way. Brody Sanders had a year round tan, a shock of hair the color of Florida sunshine, and although he wasn't a skyscraper at 5'10'', he had the build of an athlete. He dressed like he walked off the pages of a J Crew catalogue. But, it wasn't intentional, it was just Brody. Since their meeting, they were a steady date on the weekends or to parties. They each had attended the other's family events, but nothing beyond a chaste kiss or a brotherly hug had ever passed between them. Intimate talks about the future occurred often, but her daddy was right about one thing; Brody's idea of happily ever after was much closer than hers was. Lexy stopped herself; she was tying herself up in knots, and hadn't even prayed about it. The lyrics of Casting

Crowns', *Lifesong*, ran through her mind and she prayed. *Lord, please guide me through this decision. If I am supposed to be somewhere else, move me, God. As much as home means to me, it is not home unless You are by my side. Show me what to do, Jesus. In Your Name, Amen.* Lexy felt the familiar shower of peace rush over her, and even anticipated with some excitement the doors God would open and close in answer to her prayer.

Lexy was blow drying her hair when her mother peaked through the bathroom door. Lexy quickly switched the dryer off. "Hi, Mom. What's up?"

Lexy noticed that her mother looked tired, which was rare. "Mind if I talk to you while you get ready?"

"Nope. I just have to put on my makeup real quick. Is everything ok?"

Elizabeth King sat down on one of the vanity chairs, and looked down at her hands. When she looked up, Lexy could definitely see something was on her mind.

"Mom?"

"I wanted to talk to you a little about the letter from Joline Darcy."

Lexy nodded her head a bit reluctantly as she quickly grabbed her cosmetics bag from under the counter and began applying her makeup. It wasn't that she didn't want to talk to her mom; she just wanted to process everything first. But she and her mom were very close and if her mother had something to say, Lexy was willing to listen.

"We love you, baby. You know that." Lexy could see her mother's crystal blue eyes watering. "And we are so proud of you. I don't want your father's conversations with Joline to come across like we don't think you can make your own decisions. It's just that it does seem like a good opportunity, and we really want you to spread your wings a little bit, see what's out there."

Lexy stopped putting on her mascara, and looked at her mother. Her tone wasn't disrespectful, but it was tight with frustration. "Mom, you and Daddy act like I've never been outside of the city limits of Jacksonville. Have you forgotten about our vacations out west, mission trips to Haiti, remember Europe, mom? Three weeks touring the English countryside gave me *some* culture. I've hardly been sheltered."

Elizabeth nodded her head thoughtfully. "You're right, Lexy. You have had lots of blessed opportunities to travel. But that's not what we mean by spread your wings. You haven't had a chance to live on your own, without your Dad and me or your two brothers to look after your every step." Lexy started to interrupt but her mother put her hand up in protest. "Not that you've asked us to, but we've been there, regardless. I just think living away from us for a couple of months will give you a fresh perspective."

Lexy zipped up the Vera Bradley bag and placed it underneath the counter. She sat down on the countertop and faced her mom with a worried expression. "Do you think I need a new perspective?"

Elizabeth appeared deep in thought, obviously carefully choosing her words before answering her sensitive daughter. "I know from experience the most growing is done when we are out of our comfort zone, so to speak." She stood up and enveloped Lexy in a hug. "I want the best for you, as always, and so does Daddy. But sometimes when God is all you have He is all you need." Lexy fought tears as her mother took her chin in her hand. "We want you to know that He is all you need."

Lexy drove to the nearby coffee shop in a daze. Her mother's words were resonating in her heart. She did have lots of safety nets here. She had parents, grandparents, even great grandparents. Her brother, Brad, and his wife Sara lived within fifteen minutes of her parents' house and Billy, well he lived in Africa, serving as a missionary, but he would move Heaven and Earth to make sure she was ok, she knew that. Her butterflies were having a party in her stomach since the conversation with her mom; in her heart she knew her parents were right, she did need an opportunity to grow. And to actually be a director of a day camp for kids with special needs would be quite an experience; and her dad was right, it would look great on a resume. Lexy pulled into the parking lot of Starbucks and faced the only obstacle that stood between her and two months away from home, Brody.

"Augusta, Ga.! Where did that idea come from?"

Brody's face was tense as he tried to process the information. They had left their group of friends and decided to walk around the popular Town Center. He had been holding her hand but let it go to stare into the penny fountains. When he turned back to her, his face showed hurt and a little impatience. "It's because your father hates me, right?"

"No, Brody." She explained her parents' reasoning.

"And how long will you be gone?"

"About 8 weeks."

He huffed and reached for her hand. The sounds and smells of shopping surrounded them, but he looked at her like she was the only human being in the world. His tone was just short of begging. "Are you going? You could say no. You don't have to do everything they tell you to do." He looked at her hopefully.

Lexy bit her bottom lip. There were times in her life when God didn't answer her prayers for months, even years down the road, but this one He had been real quick to answer. She should go. The truth was she wanted to go. But the last thing she would ever do is hurt Brody, the boy who had respected her for more than three years, never asked for anything she wasn't willing to give. She caressed his hand in hers. "They didn't tell me to do it. I could say no. You are right."

He searched her eyes. "But?"

"But... I think I want to go. As much as I do not want to leave home or you, honestly, it is a great opportunity, and they make some valid points about being on my own for a while."

Silence hung between them for several seconds. Finally, Brody spoke. His voice was full of emotion because he knew her well enough to know she had made her decision. "I'll miss you, Lexy. Promise me something, ok?"

Lexy waited.

"Promise me you won't fall in love while you are away."

She let out a sound of nervous laughter and shook her head. "Brody…"

He cupped her cheek with his hand. "No, Lex. I mean it. We've been together for a while. I've told you my feelings for you, but you've never returned those feelings, in words anyway."

Lexy could feel her face warming. It was true. She couldn't tell Brody she loved him because she didn't know that to be true. She cared for him, very much. But love? "I'm sorry…"

His hands on her shoulders and the blueness of his pleading eyes stopped her words. "I'm not asking you to lie, Lexy. I'm just asking you to keep me close to your heart while you are gone. Don't let anyone else in. I've prayed for you, for us for a long time. It is in God's hands and I know it. But I really don't want to lose you."

The obvious contradiction in his words bothered her, but before she could respond, several of their friends caught up with them, and they ended up with the group until she got in her jeep to drive away. Brody looked at her for a long time before she finally pulled away; she knew the reason for his stare. The promise he asked for never happened. Relief flooded her with every mile she put between them; it wasn't that she was going to fall in love, but she certainly didn't want to make a promise she couldn't keep.

Chapter 2

The telephone had only rung once before the person on the other line answered with a friendly hello.

"May I speak to Dr. Darcy, please?"

"This is Dr. Darcy. How may I help you?"

Lexy swallowed hard and tried to think how to introduce herself. "Dr. Darcy, this is Lexy King…."

"Alexandra! How good to hear from you; I have heard nothing but glowing praises from your father. I trust he received my letter?"

"Yes ma'am."

"And if I know Will, you had no idea of how to make sense of the contents of that letter?"

Caught off guard at the use of her father's nickname, Lexy hesitated, then laughed. "You are correct."

"Well, honey, let me just tell you first that you would definitely be a God-send. They have turned this camp over to me, and frankly I do not have time to sort it out. The best thing I can do is delegate it to someone else. But, be sure, if this is not where you want to be this summer, don't let your father, mother, or me push you into something you don't feel led to do. Time is the most valuable gift God gives us; it shouldn't be wasted."

Lexy couldn't help but smile. She already liked this woman. "Well, actually, Dr. Darcy…"

"Child, I knew your mama and daddy when they were younger than you. I saw the promise of you and your brothers before they even got a clue. Call me Jo."

Lexy bit her bottom lip, not really comfortable calling someone her parents' age, much less her potential employer by their first name, but it already seemed strange to call this friendly person anything else. "Ok, thank you. Jo, I have prayed about it and would really like the opportunity to work with you in Augusta."

"Wonderful! We are so excited. We, meaning my cousin, Frannie and me. We are roommates and would be honored if you would live in our extra room during the time of the camp."

Lexy didn't know what to say. She didn't want to impose, but she also didn't know where else she could rent for only two months. "I don't want to be an imposition."

"Nonsense, we're two women past their prime who will live vicariously through you." Jo laughed like someone who was comfortable in her own skin. "Seriously, I don't have any biological children and Frannie's live far away. We would be thrilled to get to know you."

Lexy had to admit the short time talking to Jo gave her the feeling living with her would prove to be delightful. "Ok, well then I accept, with much gratitude."

Jo's voice held much excitement. "Outstanding. When will you arrive?"

Lexy looked at her calendar. It was May 16. According to the letter, camp began on June 6. She would need some time to get settled and organized. "Would it be too early to arrive next week?"

"That would be perfect, honey. Just perfect. School gets out on the 24th this year. We will expect you on May 28. In the meantime, tell those parents of yours thank you and to behave themselves."

"Ok, Jo. Thanks."

Lexy hung up the phone, unable to keep from smiling.

Lexy found her parents downstairs getting ready for their routine afternoon jog. Her mother was stretching and her father was bent over tying his shoes. They were shameless in their matching white and blue Nike attire; they looked like they could be on the cover of some kind of running magazine. Both their heads popped up when they heard Lexy's footsteps. "Hi."

"Hi." They both said in unison. Their expression mirrored expectation. Both of them knew she had been praying about the job for the last week, so a decision was soon to come.

"I called Dr. Darcy." Silence. Lexy decided to play with them for a bit; no need letting them off the hook too easy. Her father spoke first.

"And?"

"She's nice. Certainly seems to know a lot about the two of you."

Interestingly enough, her father's face began to turn red and her mother blushed like a school girl. After clearing his throat, her dad continued. "Yes, well I told you Joline and I go way back."

Lexy smiled and looked down, pretending to concentrate a little too hard on her nails. "Apparently so. I didn't know she knew Mom, too. Hmmmm, bet she could tell me some interesting…."

Elizabeth interrupted. "Lexy, please. What else…" She looked at William and cleared her throat. "besides your father and me did you two talk about?"

"Living arrangements."

A couple of seconds passed for added drama, but then her face broke out in a huge smile. "I accepted the job."

Both parents simultaneously hugged her, effectively cutting off her air supply.

She pulled away, flustered. "I still am not sure why you guys are so thrilled about this, but I've prayed about it and everything has worked out, so I'm game. We'll see what happens." She kissed them both and headed towards the kitchen, missing the knowing glance that passed between her parents.

Pent up tears ran rivers down Lexy's face as she drove down the Southside Connector that would eventually lead to the interstate. It wasn't that she didn't want to go, but leaving everything she knew for a couple of months was a little daunting. Homesickness was inevitable and she dreaded it. She looked at the clock on her dash. If everything went well, she would be pulling into Jo and Frannie's driveway by 7:00 p.m. She was grateful to have missed traffic, and would be well on her way by the five o'clock hour. Her bright red Jeep Wrangler was loaded to the hilt. Her father had the jeep serviced, checked, and rechecked before the departure. She had her roadside service card tucked neatly in her glove compartment along with her cell phone fully charged and programmed with every emergency and non-emergency number known to man. A small cooler full of bottled water, Diet Coke, and snacks, including plenty of chocolate sat on the passenger seat. Her mother was convinced if she didn't have to stop the danger factor of traveling alone was cut in half.

Brad and his wife had come to the house to see her off, along with Brody. Brody's goodbye was the most difficult. The last week, since her decision, he acted so insecure. He wanted her every waking minute to be spent with him. It was bizarre, because she had been away before. Granted, not for two months, but still it wasn't the first time they had been apart. But for some reason, this was different in his eyes. It was like he was sure this was the end and wanted to hold on for as long as he could. Lexy didn't understand it but her mother tried to offer some wisdom the night before she left. They were sitting in the kitchen, sharing a cup of hot tea before bed. Lexy had alluded to Brody's behavior, not that she had to, it was obvious to everyone including her two dachsunds, Sunny and Shiny. But Elizabeth got a thoughtful look on her face as she stirred some lemon into her cup of tea.

"It's hard to let go, especially when you care for someone so much."

Lexy shook her head. "But Mom, I'm not letting go of him. I'm just going away."

Her mom got a sweet smile on her face and reached out to brush back a wayward wisp of hair from Lexy's face. "Honey, I know that and in his head Brody knows that too. But we both also know that you will never be exactly the same after this trip. You are stepping out like you have never stepped out before. It scares him."

Lexy didn't comment. The truth was she couldn't. A lump had formed in her throat and she couldn't get passed it. Why was it necessary for things to change? A part of her wanted to stay safe and sound within the walls of her parents' home. She wanted to be in a relationship with a friend who never pressured her to be more than she was willing to be. If going to Augusta was going to change who she was, maybe she shouldn't go. But then, a verse came to mind, one Lexy claimed a long time ago. It was in the book of Hebrews, twelfth chapter first verse. The words of the verse had taken root in her heart and it was like her soul was giving her brain a refresher course. *"Therefore, since we are surrounded by such a great cloud of witnesses, let us throw off everything that hinders and the sin that so easily entangles, and let us run with perseverance the race marked out for us."*   As she headed towards the Georgia line, she repeated the words aloud again. If this was the race marked out for her, and she had to believe it was, then she couldn't think of anyplace else she would rather be. Right then, she decided that yes, change was inevitable; but she would cling to the one thing that never changed, her Savior and His promises.

Lexy turned up the Avalon CD and sang along. She was almost there, noting the green mileage signs dictating her progress. About an hour was all she had left. She was making good time. Lexy had truly enjoyed the trip; the change of scenery wasn't drastic but it was enough to intrigue her. In fact, she could now see slight rolling hills leading the way to Augusta. Overall, the drive had been a good one. She had done a lot of thinking and praying. The farther away she got from home, the more strength God gave her. She could feel expectation flowing through her veins and was excited about meeting Jo and Frannie. She was excited about hearing more about the camp and her responsibilities. More than anything, she was excited to meet the kids. Her father's words came back to her over and over again. *Kids who didn't belong anywhere else.*

Lexy remembered the first time she had felt called to teach kids with special needs. There was a child in children's church, Tobias, who had Down syndrome; he had a difficult time following along with transitions, so Lexy, an active member of the youth group, was paired up to aid in the process. The pairing lasted the better part of a year, and during that time Lexy fell in love, not only with little Toby, but with teaching. From that point on, she volunteered every summer working with students with disabilities. Her high school summers were filled with touching stories of inspiration and hope. Truly, she couldn't imagine doing anything else. She had almost decided to get a teaching position right out of college, but hesitated because of the direction special education was going in the public schools. Was she ready for all the challenges the job presented? She had heard some of the teachers talk in the lounge during her internships, and she couldn't help but be on the receiving end of some negativity, not only towards the profession, but potentially towards the kids. She didn't want to start out in a brand new career with a defeatist attitude, so she decided to give it some time.

Lexy looked down at the directions Jo had emailed to her the week before. Driving down Washington Road, what looked like a suburban community gradually turned to woods. Eventually, when she thought she was going to drop off the face of the earth, William Few Parkway appeared. Knob Hill, the name of Jo's subdivision, was on the left. Lexy turned into the subdivision and even though she couldn't see much in the dark, the homes looked perfectly manicured, with large yards and impeccable landscaping. Lexy made the final turn on Avrett Lane and smiled at the light brick house that stood in front of her. The white columned porch had two rocking chairs and several potted plants tastefully displayed. There was a sign on the door that read, *Sit long talk much.*

Lexy walked up the few stairs leading to the front door when it flew open and a fluffy, white poodle began attacking her tennis shoes. She couldn't help but laugh. "Hey, little girl. And who are you?" Lexy bent down to calm the excited dog, when a familiar voice from inside answered her questions. "That is just Peaches. Don't worry; her bark is bigger than her bite."

Lexy looked up to meet the person that definitely matched the voice she had come to love. She put her hand out to shake Jo's, but it was pushed out of the way with a hug. "Hi, Alexandra." She stopped and shook her head. "Lexy. Welcome. Welcome."

"Thank you." Lexy pulled back to greet the most infectious smile she had ever seen. Jo was in her mid fifties. She was a little taller than Lexy, with a shock of curly strawberry blonde hair and bright blue green eyes that held the promise of love and acceptance. Another woman, about the same age, came from the kitchen. She wore a bright yellow apron and her cheerful rounded face wore dark brown eyes and reddish brown hair, but the smile was the same. She too hugged Lexy.

"I'm Frannie, of course. It is so good to have you. How was your trip? Long, I bet. Have you eaten? Bet you haven't. Bet your sweet mama packed you snacks and told you not to stop. I know that's what I used to tell my girls…"

Joline rolled her eyes good naturedly. "Good grief, Frannie. Take a breath. Are you going to let her answer any of the questions you just asked?"

Frannie turned and stuck her tongue out at her slightly older first cousin. They both laughed as did Lexy. "Actually, I am hungry. You're right. That is exactly what my mother told me, and I always try to follow directions."

Frannie's smile showed victory as she turned to Jo. "Ha! There, you see. Right as rain. Come in the kitchen. Do you like lasagna? We have salad and bread and strawberry shortcake for dessert. Of course, you are welcome to anything in the kitchen you can find. You're not a vegetarian are you? Oh, I hope not. We like meat around here. But even if you are that's ok. I've got this cookbook I can look through to find some recipes…"

The whole time Frannie was talking Jo was making faces and mocking her busyness. They sat down to a feast and Lexy couldn't remember laughing so hard with two people she barely knew. The two cousins were exceptionally close. Apparently, they had grown up together from birth and after Frannie's husband died, it was the natural solution to not living alone. Frannie was a retired teacher and worked as a minister of preschool at their church. Lexy could see how she would be delightful to work for. Truly, the ladies were hilarious. Their home beckoned relaxation and honesty, and Lexy marveled at feeling like she had grown up here her whole life after only one hour.

Jo and Frannie's kitchen looked like something out of Southern Living Magazine. It was designed for entertaining with lots of space to move around in, long ceramic camel colored countertops, and an eat in area along with a formal dining room. The cabinets were white washed with a distressed appearance and glass and iron inlays displayed a collection of antique china. There were plants and farmhouse style pictures on top of the cabinetry. It was truly the kind of kitchen one would want to come in, pour a cup of coffee, and write in a journal or read a good book.

After the Italian feast Frannie had prepared, Lexy got the grand tour of the house. Jo had the downstairs master bedroom and bath that sat to the left of the living room. Frannie had a bedroom and bathroom on the right side of the house. There was an office that Jo welcomed her to use at her leisure. Upstairs was to be her quarters. It was a loft with a closet and full bathroom. Lexy could tell they had prepared it for her. The double bed was dressed in crisp white sheets and an eyelet coverlet. Sherbet green linen curtains hung from the one window overlooking the front yard.

"Well, what do you think? Like I said, not much, but it will work, won't it?" Lexy turned to answer Jo, but had a hard time speaking. She knew she liked the woman over the phone, but she never expected this much hospitality. The phrase, home away from home, held a suitcase full of meaning at the moment. All she could do was give both women a hug and whisper, "Thanks. It's perfect."

The cousins replied in unison, "Good.". Jo moved Lexy's suitcase by the bed. "Well, young lady, your mother and father will certainly want to know you arrived safely. Why don't you call them and then turn in for the night? Tomorrow morning, after you've rested, I'll brief you about Camp Courage and take you to the school where it will be housed." Lexy agreed, ready to unpack and turn in. She was exhausted and couldn't wait to get started on tomorrow.

Lexy stirred, and then her eyes popped open and several seconds passed before she remembered where she was. Augusta, Jo, Camp…..her nose began to take note of bacon and…..coffee! Oh, how she wanted some coffee. Quickly, she slipped on her robe and decided to peak downstairs before getting dressed. Sitting at the table reading what looked like their Bibles were both women, still in housecoats, with steaming cups of coffee sitting in front of them. Lexy decided to go back upstairs, not wanting to disturb their quiet time, but before she could act on her decision, Frannie's voice stopped her. "Lexy, honey, is that you?" Lexy closed her eyes and winced, then reluctantly stuck her head out of the door that closed her part of the house off from everyone else.

"Yes. I'm sorry. I didn't want to interrupt."

Jo spoke up. "Nonsense, Frannie and I do our devotionals over breakfast and coffee every morning. You are more than welcome to join us."

Lexy smiled. It sounded like fun to her. She always did a morning devotional, but she enjoyed it at home when one of her parents was around so she could bounce some of her thoughts off of them. "Thanks. I'll be right back." She ran up the stairs as the older women smiled at one another.

"Frannie, when is the last time you bounded up a flight of stairs like that?"

Frannie smiled over the rim of her cup. "Oh, I'd say about the last time you did."

Both women giggled as Lexy entered the room with her Bible and notebook in hand. "Do you mind if I get a cup of coffee?"

Frannie beamed and made a fist in victory. "Yes! Another coffee drinker. How do you like it, Lexy? I'm getting up to refill mine."

"Cream and sugar, but you don't have to wait on me."

Frannie didn't look back, but waved her hands in the air. "I know. After today, you're on your own. Promise. How about some Belgian waffles and bacon? Oh and some homemade syrup, and strawberries...."

Jo rolled her eyes and whispered to Lexy. "Just say yes; it makes life a lot easier."

Frannie peaked her head out of the pantry. "I heard that."

Jo directed her next comments to Lexy. She pointed towards her journal and devotional. "What are you studying, Lexy? Frannie and I have been working through the Psalms and Proverbs together."

Lexy smiled at the coincidence. "Actually, I've been studying Proverbs 31."

A smile spread across Jo's face as her eyebrows raised and she looked over Lexy's head to Frannie. "The virtuous woman." She looked back at Lexy. "Tall order, don't you think?"

"Yes, it is. But I've been blessed with a couple of good models in my lifetime. I think the key to the whole thing is grace and obedience."

Frannie sat a cup of coffee and a mile high plate of food in front of Lexy, then resumed her position. "That's an interesting combination. What do you mean?"

Lexy took a sip of her steaming hot coffee before responding. "Well, you need grace to have the relationship with God in the first place. And once the motivation is in place; by motivation I guess I mean the love you have for Him, then obedience is possible."

"Hmmm." Jo was flipping to the passage of scripture in her Bible, apparently thinking what Lexy had said. Frannie had followed suit and was also rereading verses 10-31. Jo looked at Lexy. "What is your favorite verse in the description?"

"My favorite? Well, I'm not married and have no children so much of it I can't relate to, yet. I understand some of it from watching my mom and grandmothers. I really like verses 25 and 26, 'She is clothed with strength and dignity; she can laugh at days to come. She speaks with wisdom, and faithful instruction is on her tongue.', but the one I repeat to myself often is verse 30."

Jo and Frannie both read the verse silently and then looked up at Lexy with expressions of approval. Jo proceeded to read the verse aloud. "Charm is deceptive, and beauty is fleeting; but a woman who fears the Lord is to be praised." She stopped and reached a hand out to Lexy, patting it like a long lost aunt. "I don't know about you, Frannie, but I wish I had possessed some of this young woman's wisdom when I was her age."

Lexy heard Frannie huff and then felt her kick Joline under the table. "I think you need to wish for some of this young woman's wisdom now, dear Joline."

Jo feigned a look of shock and then bust out laughing, as did Lexy and Frannie. After another thirty minutes of discussion and a final prayer to begin the day, Jo broached the subject of the day's agenda. "Well, Lexy, I could stay here all day in my pajamas and hold Bible study, but if we are going to be Proverbs 31 women, we have a job to do. Why don't you go upstairs and get dressed and we'll drive over to my office and go over the details of the camp?"

Lexy washed her cup out and rinsed her plate, grabbed her Bible and journal, and bounded up the stairs, saying, "I can hardly wait. Sounds great to me."

Frannie was washing the few dishes left in the sink. She didn't look up, but Joline heard her say, "I like her."

Jo smiled to herself while cleaning up her space. "Me too, Frannie, me too."

Chapter 3

Lexy was settled in the passenger seat of Jo's cornflower blue VW bug, listening to the radio, not believing how excited she was to get started on her new job. She was enjoying the view of her new surroundings in the light of day. Her dad was right; this was a beautiful place. It was green, a lot like Florida, but there were slight hills, almost like waves. She looked over at Jo who was singing along to a praise and worship song unashamedly. Her rich tenor voice was pleasant; Lexy assumed she probably sang in the choir at church. She wanted to ask questions about the actual town, but hated to interrupt. As if sensing her curiosity, Jo turned down the radio and looked over at her. "So, what do you think?" She motioned to the view that surrounded them.

"It's really pretty, Jo. Are we actually in Augusta?"

Jo shook her head. "No, technically this is Evans. It runs into Martinez; then Augusta. We're not far, though. Maybe three or four miles. People generally refer to this area along with Aiken and North Augusta as the Central Savannah River Area or CSRA. Augusta is Richmond County; Martinez and Evans are Columbia County. There are ten elementary schools, six middle schools, and five high schools that serve Columbia County."

Lexy listened quietly, truly interested by the information. In fact, surprise crossed her face when Jo laughed and glanced at her. "Listen to me, going on like Frannie. I have become what I have mocked."

"No, Jo. I want to learn as much as I can about this area. Really."

Jo smiled and nodded.

Soon, they pulled up to a beautiful stately brick structure, labeled Columbia County Board of Education. Jo whipped into a parking spot near the front doors labeled *Dr. Joline Darcy*. She rolled her eyes as she looked at Lexy. "Pretentious, is it not?"

Lexy laughed. "The building or the parking space?"

The mischievous grin Lexy had grown to love in the last 12 hours crossed the older woman's face. "Both." Jo grabbed her briefcase from the backseat. "Come on, I'll give you the grand tour." As they walked up the winding walkway, Lexy noted the sweltering heat. She was thankful for her sleeveless shirt and shorts at the moment, but even dressed for summer, it was hot. She looked at her watch—9 a.m. Not a good sign. In Florida, the heat was intense but there was always a breeze. This heat was damp, like a wet rag had been draped as an invisible canopy. Jo unlocked the double glass doors and led the way through the lobby to a hallway lined with offices. As they were approaching the third door on the right, a rather large lady with a sour expression met them as she was entering another office.

Jo turned and smiled, "Elaine, excuse me a moment." Elaine turned, her expression not changing.

When she didn't respond verbally, Jo cleared her throat and continued. "Let me introduce you to Lexy King. Lexy this is Elaine James." Jo turned back towards Lexy. "Lexy is going to be running Camp Courage this summer."

Lexy fidgeted a bit as Elaine took in her diminutive 5 foot 3 3/4 inch frame. A huff escaped her throat as she uttered, "Good luck with that. Hope they don't eat you alive."

Lexy stood with her mouth hanging open as the office door slammed in both their faces. Jo shrugged and guided Lexy across the hall to her own office. Lexy shut the door behind her. "Sorry about that, Lexy. Elaine is one of those people who is highly intelligent but has no social common sense whatsoever. Secretly, I don't think she is a very happy person."

No kidding, Lexy thought to herself. "What does she do?"

Jo was head deep in a filing cabinet trying to locate something. Her muffled voice answered Lexy. "Elaine is the assistant superintendent in charge of curriculum."

Lexy's eyebrows lowered in confusion. "I thought you were the assistant superintendent."

Jo surfaced from the depths of the cabinet, shutting it with a thud. She had a thick file in her hand so Lexy assumed her hunt had been successful. "I am. Columbia County is rather large, so more than one is needed. I'm in charge of discipline and special education. Now about the camp….let me see…" Lexy waited as Jo shuffled through the hundreds of papers stuffed in the file. She looked around the office and noted it was the perfect combination of professional and homey. The framed photos of family members, teacher type knick knacks and tasteful silk flower arrangements were an extension of Jo's home, but the dark woods and framed diplomas reminded Lexy of the pristine appearance of her father's office. Jo's voice interrupted her observation. "Ok, here you go."

Lexy reached forward and took the stapled stack of papers from Jo's hand. She skimmed the first page, trying to comprehend what she was holding. Jo came to the rescue with information. "That is the enrollment sheet for this year's camp. The list contains the students' names, ages, behavior plans and medical needs. You won't see their disabilities listed because of confidentiality reasons. There is also a budget attached, along with a list of supplies you will need. Information about day activities they have done in the past should be there as well."

Lexy looked through the first few pages of names, and noted the ages. There must have been some kind of mistake. The ages listed ranged from three years old to twenty-one. She voiced her concern to Jo who quickly informed her. "Yes. That's right. The ages of the camp correspond with ages served through federal services."

The excitement that had filled Lexy's spirit was now mixing with anxiety. There were at least a hundred students on the list whose behaviors went from mild disobedience to what some might call bizarre. There were several who required major assistance during restroom times and even two who needed catheters. How in the world was she going to serve all of those students? Thankfully, she saw a list of volunteers with phone numbers. There must have been about 25 names on the list.

Jo came around her desk and looked over her shoulder. "Good. I was hoping that was attached." She took a seat beside Lexy and handed her a steno pad and pencil.

"Here. You'll want to take notes."

Lexy placed the packet of information on the floor beside her chair and quickly poised to write.

"Camp Courage is only about five years old. Students with disabilities that affect their ability to attend a mainstreamed camp are considered for acceptance. There are actually quite a few students in the county who fit that description. It is held at alternating schools each year. This year it will be at Central High School. You are welcome to use the office facilities, along with the gym, athletic fields, cafeteria, etc. I will try to get my hands on a summer schedule so you will be aware of any events that may conflict with the camp. As you know, the camp is a 6 week program running from 9 a.m. until 2 p.m. each day. Parents are responsible for transporting their children to and from camp. Several of the children take medicine and you alone will be responsible for collecting and administering medication during the day. We'll make sure you get the appropriate release forms in order to do that. In the past the director set up groups of ten children and assigned them a teacher volunteer along with two assistants. They rotated centers each day and usually a big weekly activity was scheduled, such as bowling, the movies, hay ride, cooking, etc. You'll need to make sure the volunteers understand their responsibilities and supervise the rotating of the centers."

Lexy knew her eyes were as round as saucers when she looked up, thinking that Jo would never decide to take a breath. Jo smiled warmly, reached over and squeezed her hand. "Don't worry. You'll handle it. You've got a week before the campers arrive. I'll take you over to the school tomorrow morning. You can spend the day there, and I'm sure you'll feel better once you've acclimated yourself to the surroundings." Lexy nodded, hoping she was right.

Jo got up from her chair and began to gather her things. "Come on, kiddo. I'll treat you to lunch."

Lexy followed, not really feeling like eating, more like pouring over the papers and her notes, trying to get organized. But maybe a little food would help her take a deep breath and enjoy the moment. Was this what her parents meant by spreading her wings?

Jo drove them to a popular coffee shop for sandwiches and salad. While they were eating, several people stopped to say hi to Jo; she politely took the time to introduce her new housemate/employee. One gentleman in particular lingered at the table a little longer than the rest. His name was Robert Smitty; he was about Jo's age, and if Lexy wasn't mistaken had a flirtatious twinkle in his eye aimed in Jo's direction. After he left the table, Lexy realized her thoughts showed on her face because Jo waved a hand in the air as if brushing Mr. Smitty off. "Don't be silly. Bobby would flirt with a light pole if it had a skirt on. Actually, he is very charming, as he should be as one of the most popular attorneys in the CSRA."

Lexy nodded her head, enjoying the easy conversation that flowed between them. As she swallowed the last bite of her chicken salad sandwich, Lexy placed her napkin on her plate and asked something she had been wanting to ask since their first phone conversation a couple of weeks prior. "Jo, tell me about my mom and dad. You said you knew them while they were dating."

Jo's eyes danced. "Actually, I first knew them when they despised one another."

Lexy almost spit her sweet tea across the table. "Despised each other? My parents are such a strong alliance it is impossible slip anything by on them."

"Well, I'm sure they are a strong alliance now. They have matured as we all do, darlin'. But back then, well Lizzie and Will were the two most bull-headed people on the planet and they butted heads often, even at the altar if I remember correctly."

Lexy jumped up and down, feeling like a six year old. "Do tell, Jo, please…."

Jo only hesitated for a second. "Ok, you know my older brother, Jimmy. I'm assuming your dad has mentioned him, right?"

Lexy nodded. She had heard stories of Jimmy associated with her dad's college years forever.

"Jimmy and your dad were two years behind me in school. They were stuck together like glue and annoying as all get out. I did my best to ignore them both, but constant pranking made it impossible. You would think that a younger brother would want to steer clear of his big sister, but no, not them. You see, I was a resident assistant in an all girl's dorm. Let's just say, they came up with more excuses to visit me along with the thirty freshman girls I supervised than a sixth grader whose dog had eaten his homework."

Lexy couldn't help but laugh, picturing her prestigious father as a girl crazy eighteen year old. Jo continued. "Well, as you could probably guess, your mother was one of the girls in my dorm."

"No way!"

Jo smiled. "Yes, way! Prettiest thing you've ever seen…." Jo examined Lexy's face for a moment. "Well, now that I think about it, you do see her every time you look in the mirror. Except for your dark hair and eyes, you look just like her."

Lexy could feel her face warm at the compliment. She was often told she was a perfect mix between her parents, and secretly she loved hearing it, even though she thought her mother with her golden blonde curly hair and beautiful blue eyes was ten times more attractive than she was.

Jo continued. "So, Lizzie lived a few doors down from me; and was always surprisingly mature for her age, in a good way. She wasn't a partier and was very committed to her studies. When your father and Jimmy came around, she would make excuses to leave the premises because their sophomoric attitudes got on her last nerve. Well, at first, the two boys decided she was the biggest snob they had ever met. But then something happened to Will."

Lexy's voice was a dramatic whisper. "What happened to him?"

Jo shrugged her shoulders. "I don't know, but one day he grew up. Apparently, he worked on a project in political science and fell in love with the legal profession. The pranks stopped and whenever I saw him with Jimmy, he always had his nose in a book. Actually, he became the male version of Lizzie."

"So how did they finally hook up?"

"God stepped in, my dear."

"How so?"

"They ended up in the same sociology class. About mid semester, they were the two top performing students in the class." Jo's voice lowered to a stage whisper. "In case you don't know, both of them have a competitive streak a mile wide."

Lexy had never thought of her parents as competitive, but then remembered all their marathons, half marathons, and tennis matches she had attended in her life.

"They couldn't stand it when one would out perform the other. Sensing this, the wise sociology guru, paired the two up for a weighty project. I imagine he sat back and laughed watching them attempt to work together. He probably used them as research for some article he was writing. Anyway, all the time, I either had to listen to one or the other complain about the obnoxious something or other the other one said or did. The whole time I knew they were falling in love. Don't ask me how, but I just knew."

"So what happened?"

"They submitted their project and failed miserably."

"What?!"

Jo laughed as she finished the last of her lemonade. "Yep! They were both so consumed with outdoing each other, they completely missed the objective of the project. Failed, F. But again, the wise professor was greatly amused at the behavior of his two star students. He gave them a chance to do it over."

"So…"

"They worked on it diligently for two weeks and submitted it the day of the final. They ended up acing it."

"What happened after that?"

"They were engaged one month later."

Lexy sat back in her seat, completely amused at the story. She said more to herself than to Jo, "And were you serious about them butting heads at the altar?"

Jo rolled her eyes. "Oh, yes. If I remember correctly, they had a disagreement over who would say their vows first. It was during the rehearsal and the poor preacher just kept looking back and forth between the two of them, probably thinking this was the last time they would ever stand at the altar together. Lizzie ended up trying to take her engagement ring off and throw it at Will, but it was stuck and wouldn't come off her finger. They ended up laughing so hard they could barely speak, and soon all was forgiven."

Lexy shook her head. Unbelievable. She had lived with her parents all her life, and didn't even know whole chunks of their past. "I wonder why they've never told me all this before."

Jo smiled as she gathered up her trash. "Have you ever asked?"

Thinking about it, Lexy realized she hadn't. She guessed she assumed they had been together forever. "No."

Jo left the tip on the table and stood up to leave. "Well, there you go. Now you know your beginnings…"

Lexy smiled to herself and followed. "Yeah, you're right. I guess I do."

Lexy walked up the breezeway to Central High School ready to begin piecing together the schedule of activities for the camp. She and Jo had only enough time to drive to the campus yesterday, but didn't actually view the facilities. The night before, after a meal of homemade chicken pot pie and peach cobbler topped with ice-cream, Lexy waddled up the flight of stairs and spread the paper work in front of her and began organizing the names into groups based on age and behavioral tendencies. She also called most of the volunteers on the list and confirmed 23 of the 25. She talked briefly to the teachers and found out their area of preference. After three hours she was satisfied with the dent she had made, and turned in for the night. She was refreshed by a light breakfast (Frannie had to be at work early.) and a short devotional time with Jo and Frannie. After showering, throwing on a pair of khaki shorts, a blue tank top, and pushing her dark curly hair back with a headband, she was ready to tackle the day. Her main agenda for her first day in the school would be to plan the activities, take an inventory, and go shopping. Luckily, most of the major shopping in Evans was on one long strip of road; so hopefully, she wouldn't get lost easily.

As she unlocked the glass doors to the school, she noticed very few lights were on. She recalled seeing only an old pickup truck in the parking lot along with a van, marked Masters Cleaners. She wasn't worried though. Jo mentioned there would only be a few people in the building this week. Even the secretaries were on vacation until a couple of weeks into Camp Courage. Although Lexy would love to meet some new people, she supposed the lack of distraction would help her get some things accomplished. Lexy followed the signs to the office and turned on a couple of lights. There were two secretary's desks in the front section leading to a long hallway lined with offices. Most of the offices were labeled, *Principal, Assistant Principal, Counselor,* etc. Lexy found the teacher's lounge, noted the couch, work table and vending machines, and decided she had found home base, for the week, anyway. Jo said one of the offices would be available for her use during the duration of the camp; but she felt more comfortable camping out in a public area; the idea of invading someone's space didn't feel right to her. She spread out her paperwork on the long table and began to make a list of what she would need. After what seemed like an hour, she grabbed her pad and pencil and decided to take a tour of the facilities to see what she already had at her disposal.

Several minutes of wandering around blindly ticked by before she found her way to the home economics room. She turned on the lights, noted the number of tables and chairs, and then looked at the kitchen facility. One of the refrigerators was labeled Camp Courage. Lexy opened it to see it had been cleaned out for her use. There were plenty of cooking utensils, bowls, and pots. There was a range and oven, along with a plethora of other appliances and kitchen gadgets. She would have to buy the food for the snacks; she made a note to watch out for food allergies when shopping. Luckily, the campers brought their own lunches.

Satisfied with her tour of the kitchen, she headed to the gym. Looking around, she saw a sign that pointed towards the end of the building. Funny, she smelled the gym before she actually saw it. Why was it that all gyms smelled the same, like old socks and cleaning chemicals? It was fairly dark, but Lexy could make out the courts, bleachers and several championship flags for various sports. It was certainly big enough to accommodate her campers during free play and game centers. Next, she needed to find the equipment room to see if there were balls,

Frisbees, hula hoops, and maybe some other interesting games available for her use. She saw what looked like a corridor of offices and headed that way. Lexy found the weight room, which was locked and across the hall was a sign that read Athletic Director. She knocked but no one answered. Next to it was another door. She tried the handle; it was open. She smiled as she surveyed the contents of the room, Bingo; she found it. Although it was a mess, there were all types of equipment. She waded into the sea of rackets, balls, and nets when she heard someone approaching. Thinking it was a janitor doing his or her job, she didn't lift her head, just concentrated on things to add to her list.

"What do you think you're doing?!"

Lexy tried to turn around but tripped on her own shoes as she attempted to locate the source of the rather rude voice behind her.

As soon as she found her footing, she realized she was staring at someone's chest. Whoever it was loomed over her by several inches, maybe even a foot. She looked up to see him staring at her, arms crossed.

Lexy attempted to back up and regain some personal space but the cluttered mess trapped her. So, instead she straightened herself and tried to regain some dignity in what looked like to be someone who didn't appreciate her presence very much. "Hello. My name is…"

The grumpy giant cut her off as he backed up. "How did you get in here?"

Well, so much for introductions. Lexy couldn't keep the defensiveness out of her voice. "The door was unlocked."

He wore sunglasses, a hat and a whistle around his neck. She assumed he was a coach or maybe the athletic director, although he did look a little young to hold an administrative position. "Like I was trying to say before, my name is Lexy King."

He took off his sunglasses and immediately Lexy felt her heart skip a beat. He had the most intense green eyes she had ever seen. They were beautiful, as was he. Whoever he was appeared to be at least six feet tall, big and burly with muscular legs, and what looked like could be a great smile if it weren't distorted in the grizzly grimace.

The harsh tone that spewed out of his mouth confirmed her assessment.

"Whoever you are, you need to stay out of my equipment room. There are procedures about using this stuff, and if you need anything, fill out a form and I'll see about it when I get time." His stare challenged her to say something in return.

She was sure her mouth was hanging open. She had never been spoken to like that in her life. If her brothers were here, they would disregard the giant's size and pummel him anyway for talking to their baby sister like she was some kind of child who broke into a forbidden treasure. Well, her brothers weren't here, but she still intended to defend herself. But before she could say a word, the giant put on his sunglasses and turned, leaving the room.

"This day just keeps on getting better and better." David mumbled the words under his breath as he stormed into his office, grabbed his clipboard, and slammed the door before going onto the field.

First, the booster club president had the audacity to come and talk to him about last season's failures. Obviously, it didn't matter that David was spending all of his time preparing to make a bunch of boys who would rather be playing video games into men with character, one being the booster president's son. Then, he got a call from a parent asking why the weight room over at a neighboring high school was more equipped than theirs was. Hindsight being 20/20, he should have handed the phone to the president of the booster club and let him explain that one. On the tails of the disgruntled parent, his mother calls to say his little brother, Tommy, had been admitted to the hospital for another lung treatment to control his horrid bouts with Cystic Fibrosis. The thought of his brother hooked up to breathing machines while someone beat on his back to loosen the grip of the death provoking mucus made him sick. And to top it all off, he sees that woman plundering through the stack of equipment he still had not the time or assistance to organize. She was probably a new cheerleading coach or some such nonsense. That's all he needed was one more woman flittering around him trying to make his life miserable.

David brooded towards the football field and surveyed the progress of his landscaping mission in the midst of another scorching hot summer. The grass was definitely fried; it wasn't getting enough water. The sigh that escaped his throat betrayed frustration. He had been working on the appearance of the weight room and other facilities with minimal assistance from his coaching staff. Even though he knew the four dedicated men who worked with him would gladly help, he hated to ask any of them to take even more time away from their wives and kids to work in a situation where they got paid the equivalent of ten cents an hour for their intense efforts. David was looking at the end zone trying to envision the painting of a new hawk, when a thud knocked him in the head. He looked down to see a football rolling at his feet; he expected to look up and find some smart alleck kid coming towards him or one of his coaches trying to play a joke, but instead the woman from the equipment room was storming towards him with a look of fury on her face.

"What are you doing?!" He was rubbing his head, more amazed by the fact she had to have thrown the football from twenty yards away to hit him with that much force. Now that they were in the light of day, he was alarmed to realize he might be dealing with a student. The little person standing in front of him was at best 5'3'', maybe 100 pounds, with no makeup and a sprinkle of freckles across a ski slope nose. She appeared to be maybe seventeen. He couldn't finish processing her appearance, because when she reached him, she actually thumped his arm.

"I am trying to get your attention, in case you didn't notice."

He looked at her, not blinking. Her efforts had worked. This must be what shock felt like. "By hitting me with a football?"

Her voice raised a notch. "Yes. Obviously, civilized manners don't work with you. What is your name?"

He could barely speak. She must have some kind of mental issue, maybe he should tread lightly. "Coach Griffin. David Griffin. Look, Miss…"

Lexy held up her hand to silence him. "No. I've heard what you have to say. Now you can hear me out. My name is Alexandra King. I was hired to direct Camp Courage. It is housed at your school. Maybe you haven't heard of it, but I really don't care. I am from out of town, and have no idea what the procedures are for checking things out. But my boss, Dr. Darcy, told me I could come up here and try to get organized before camp. I was trying to make a list of things I had access to before I went to shop for new supplies. I was looking for equipment and found it. Now if you want me to fill out paperwork to check out some balls and a couple of hula hoops tell me where the form is and I will be more than happy to do so."

David started to speak but then realized she wasn't done yet. Her hands had quit flailing around and had landed squarely on her tiny hips. "I don't know who you think you are, or where you were raised, but you should try using some manners…"

He had heard enough. It was time to silence the little lady's tirade. "You're right. I am sorry. I was rude." He tried not to smile as she apparently attempted to straighten out her posture to maybe reach 5'4'' tall.

Her chin jutted up in the air as she said, "thank you" and turned on her heal and actually began what looked like a victory march back to the school.

When she got about twenty five yards away, he yelled, "Hey, Ms.King! You forgot something."

She turned, poised for a fight, but instead was apparently shocked to see a flying ball coming towards her. David was impressed as he watched her assess the situation, catch the ball effortlessly and continue on her path. He turned towards the war bird behind him and couldn't help but smile. For the first time in a long time, his efforts to concentrate on his work were ruined by an irresistible urge to laugh.

Chapter 4

Lexy saw red as she pulled out of the school parking lot. She made an effort to concentrate on the rest of her agenda but the arrogant giant of a jerk on the football field sabotaged her focus. All she could think about was his smug expression as he apologized to her. When she thought about him leaving the equipment room after he bit her head off, not even giving her a chance to speak, much less apologize, it sent her reeling. True, she probably shouldn't have hit him with the football, and the thumping was also not a very lady like gesture; in fact she could hear her mother's reprimand, "Alexandra Lynne!" but at the same time she also could see the satisfied expressions of her father and brothers. Regardless, Coach Griffin had definitely ruined her first day on the job. Mentally exhausted, she decided to put off shopping until the next day and head to Jo's for a light lunch and maybe even a jog around her new neighborhood. Realizing she was the only one home, Lexy quickly unloaded her car, ate a granola bar and half a grapefruit and headed out the door to run. Despite her day, the idea of jogging through a new setting excited her. She set her ipod on the praise and worship track, and gradually felt the tension leave her body; soon her mind was not on David Griffin, but on thanking God for her blessings instead. After about 45 minutes she climbed the stairs to her loft much lighter than she had before, and after a shower and a 15 minute power nap she was a new woman. Lexy was knee deep in planning the camp when she heard a soft knock on her door.

She looked up and glanced at the digital clock on her nightstand; it was almost five o'clock. "Come in."

Jo peaked her head in the door, and it drew an automatic smile from Lexy. "You look awfully pretty today, Jo." And she did. Maybe pretty wasn't exactly the right word; sophisticated was better. After only seeing her in lounging clothes or casual capris, the sight of her in a navy tailored suit and a crisp white shirt made her realize her hostess was one that undoubtedly commanded respect when she entered a room.

Jo sat on the bed watching Lexy hover over her papers. "Well thank you, my dear. Normally, I don't dress this way during the summer, but I had a meeting about the budget with the principals today." She actually stuck her tongue out. "No fun. But….come to think of it, the day wasn't all boring. I got a rather….entertaining phone call." Lexy looked up from her paperwork at Jo's pause. "By chance, were your ears burning today?"

A look of confusion crossed Lexy's face. "No. Why?" She sat up, alarmed. "Oh, no. Have I already done something wrong?"

Jo's smile was mischievous as she shook her head and waggled her eyebrows. "Nooooooo. Nothing wrong. It's just that your father failed to mention you had such amazing catching and throwing…." Lexy closed her eyes in horror as Jo cleared her throat and continued, "and thumping abilities."

Lexy covered her face with her hands, but peaked through her fingers to see Jo's amused expression. "How did you find out about all that?"

"David called me."

Lexy jumped up and stood over Jo like she had grown three heads. "What? Are you telling me that jerk called to tattle tale on me like….like… some overgrown child?"

Jo's expression betrayed humor. "Oh my. He did make quite an impression, didn't he? David actually called to apologize to me. It seems that once he found out I hired you he felt really bad about the whole misunderstanding."

Lexy sat down on her bed and placed her head in her hands. When she looked up at Jo, she couldn't help but grimace. "Huh. Misunderstanding? A chance to understand would have been something I would have welcomed." She thought a second. "I don't know if I want to hear the answer to this question, but why would David call you to apologize?"

Jo smiled, the kind of motherly smile that made Lexy want to break down and cry. "I hired David five years ago, and let's just say he and I have a different kind of relationship."

"What do you mean?"

Jo moved across the room and sat beside Lexy. "David's almost like a son. Granted, one that misbehaves at times, but still he has some good qualities." Lexy could feel her lunch sitting like a lump in her stomach, but she listened. "Like I said, I hired David about five years ago. He came to me looking for employment and needed to know how to get certified in Georgia. He lived in South Carolina at the time." She shook her head, "Let me back up a little bit. David's girlfriend lived in this area. She was a real estate agent, I think. Anyway, the two had met in college and dated a while. David proposed and they decided when they married it would be best for them to live in Augusta. So, that is when I met him. We had just lost a coach at Central and needed a replacement. David had the credentials, not to mention an impressive coaching record, especially for being so young, so he just fit."

Lexy noticed the sadness in Jo's eyes. "Why do I get the feeling that's not the end of the story?"

"Unfortunately, it isn't." She continued. "Right after David started working at Central, a new cheerleading coach was hired. I think her name was Becky. From all reports, Becky set her sights for David the moment she saw him, fiancée or not. She would shamelessly flirt with him, but then get upset when the affections were not returned. Well, one day David sat her down in his classroom and tried to mend the situation. He told her he loved his fiancée and had no intentions of doing anything that would jeopardize the relationship; plus, David claimed to be a Christian and fooling around was not part of his calling card. Apparently Becky left irate and embarrassed."

Lexy grimaced. "I imagine so."

"Well, she was so upset she ended up accusing David of sexual harassment to try to get him fired. Instead of what really happened in his classroom, she reported that he tried to make a pass at her and got angry when she did not return his affections. No one at school believed her, but nevertheless her lie almost cost David his career."

Lexy couldn't believe a human being could be so calculating. "So what happened?"

"God intervened."

Regardless of her not so pleasant encounter with the burly coach, Lexy sat up, hoping the outcome was good. "How so?"

"Right before David and Becky had their talk a student had completed a presentation. The video camera was left on and it actually recorded the whole incident. David discovered it right before he was going to be asked to take a break, so to speak."

"You mean the school was actually going to let him go? They believed her?"

"No, not really. But, unfortunately when a woman cries sexual harassment the mere appearance of impropriety sends school officials running for the hills. They were going to ask him to take a leave of absence until the whole ordeal could be worked out."

"But then he was cleared?"

"Yes. He was cleared. He was even promoted to Athletic Director. But David grew bitter. It didn't help his fiancée broke up with him during the time of the accusation. He has never quite been the same since."

Lexy thought a moment. She felt for him, she really did. But his behavior towards her was still completely unwarranted. "It still doesn't give him the right to be rude…"

Jo put her hand on Lexy's shoulder. "No, honey, it doesn't. But he does have a lot on his mind. As AD of a large high school, he gets lots of pressure from the board and the boosters." Lexy looked at Jo and could see something else about David was troubling her.

Lexy's sigh was audible. "What else, Jo?"

Jo's voice grew soft. "There's Tommy."

"Who's Tommy?"

"Tommy is David's little brother. He's only 15 years old and has Cystic Fibrosis. He's been in and out of hospitals since birth and the doctors don't think he is going to make it past his 18th birthday."

Lexy could feel the tears gathering in her eyes. She had studied about CF in college and knew the mortality rate was not good. She couldn't imagine losing one of her siblings at all, much less at such a young age. Suddenly, she felt horrible about the way she had handled herself and said so. "So I guess I shouldn't have hit him with the football, huh?"

Jo put her arm around Lexy's shoulders. "No, I wouldn't say that. It sounds like he needed someone to knock him around a bit." She looked in her eyes, much like her mother would. "I just thought you should know the whole story."

Jo patted her on the knee and got up to leave. "I'll see you for dinner. Frannie's making her famous meatloaf and mashed potatoes."

"Hey, Jo?"

She turned around to face Lexy.

"Thanks." Jo smiled and closed the door behind her.

Lexy inherited the high achieving, to do list kind of personality from both parents. William and Elizabeth King had always approached every day with an organized plan in the form of a list. Whether it be scratched on a piece of paper or on one of her mother's monogrammed notepads, the list was the gauge of how each day was progressing. When the list was completed, it was time to kick back and bask in the productivity of the day. If the list was not completed, the day was not as good and the unchecked items carried over to the next day. This list making genetic link carried over to all three children.

Some would argue it is learned behavior, but Lexy firmly believed it was part of her biological make up. She knew this because in college she found out not every one had the natural inclination to be a list maker. Her college roommate, Zoe, who she dearly loved, thought Lexy was on the borderline of suffering from Obsessive Compulsive Disorder. She even challenged Lexy to go one week without a list. Lexy made it through one morning, and decided she was going to have a nervous breakdown if she didn't start literally checking something off.

So, it was with great joy that she sat in the Central High School cafeteria on Friday morning before camp surrounded by her faithful volunteers explaining what had been accomplished on the to do list dictating the preparations for Camp Courage. Out of the 25 volunteers, 22 had shown up. She had ten certified teachers, nine women and one man, all of which would be drawing a small salary, and ten middle school to college aged true volunteers who would act as their assistants. Plus, she had a music teacher, Mrs. Jackson, and an art teacher, Ms. Mason, who would assist with those two centers. All she needed was someone to supervise activities in the gym and her world would be perfect. Lexy looked at her workers and suddenly got a little emotional; they were all excited, and willing, and able which was so much more than she had prayed for. She knew some of them thought she was taking on a daunting task being so young and handling what was a very large day camp, but their smiles and attentive nods spoke volumes of their encouragement towards her.

"I want to thank all of you for showing up today and listening to my ramblings about the nuts and bolts of the daily activities. I know that we'll run into some snags when the actual campers show up, but I trust that being as prepared as possible will put out some potential fires. So.....that being said, I'll see you on Monday."

The group started chatting pleasantly as Lexy gathered the forms she had collected together and placed them in her tabbed notebook. She looked at her list posted on the front of her notebook and checked off staff meeting. The next item was to go to the office and set up camp at a central location so checking in on Monday would not be a major headache. As she loaded all her materials in her dollar store plastic crate, she could feel a looming presence behind her. When she turned to investigate, her nose met the emblem on a sky blue polo shirt. She closed her eyes briefly recognizing the imposing wall of a man, and then stepped back so she could look fully into David the Giant's face.

"Excuse me."

She swallowed hard, trying not to allow the mere sight of him in his khaki shorts and form fitting shirt to render her speechless. Since the talk with Jo earlier in the week, Lexy had been convicted to do some serious praying when it came to her attitude towards the surly coach. She told herself to forget the situation and move on. Lexy had avoided him like the plague during the past few days, but she felt like she actually owed him an apology, which was not something she was jumping up and down to do. "Can I help you?" Inwardly, she winced at the shakiness of her voice.

His perfect teeth showed themselves in the form of what looked like, could it actually be, the hint of a humble smile? The fact that he almost seemed in pain as he offered some sort of friendliness amused her—a little. "Yes. I, um, would actually like to first, apologize for the other day, again."

Lexy met his gaze full on. "Accepted." *Ok, here goes Lord. I hope this is what You want me to do.* She knew it was. "And I owe you an apology for....well, physically and verbally assaulting you."

Some of his nervousness faded away in the relaxation of his posture and the twinkling in his eyes. "Accepted....I would also like to volunteer."

"To do what?"

He laughed. *Wow*, she thought. *That was nice.* "Work the camp. I heard you needed someone to supervise the gym's activities."

Oh...he wants to keep an eye on his territory. Well, she did need somebody. Why not?

Lexy shrugged her shoulders in an effort to be nonchalant. "Ok, Coach Griffin. Sure, that would be great."

"Call me David."

"Ok, David."

He stood there looking at her like there was something else on his mind. After a few awkward seconds and some shuffling of feet on her part, she ventured, "Is there anything else?"

"Yes. My brother, Tommy. He would like to volunteer the last couple of weeks of camp. He's from out of town, but will be staying with me before he returns to school in the fall."

Lexy placed the crate that was getting heavier by the second, on the table beside her. She debated on asking if enrolling Tommy as a camper would be more appropriate, but she realized he didn't know of her knowledge about the situation. What could it hurt? If it proved to be too much for Tommy, he could always fall into one of the groups. "Ok, just write down his name for me and I will add him to the list for the last couple of weeks." Her heart softened as she saw David relax a little bit more. "Will that work?"

"Yes, and Ms. King?"

"Lexy."

Another unbelievable smile as he reached out to shake her hand. She quickly responded hoping hers wasn't as clammy as it felt. "Lexy. Thank you."

She held his gaze and his handshake. "You're welcome."

David went back to his office, rapid heartbeat and all. What was he doing? True, Alexandra, Lexy, was cute, even pretty if he was really honest with himself. True, the speech she gave the camp workers seemed very sweet and genuine. True, she had to be very special if Jo had hired her. But most true, she was a woman, and women had taken his heart and almost his career, too.

When he talked to his mother and begged for Tommy to come spend some time with him, he immediately thought of Camp Courage and even volunteering to be a part of something with his much younger brother. But Lexy's position as director stopped him. The truth was he couldn't stop thinking about her since their encounter on the football field. He had never met anyone with such small stature and larger than life spirit. Even Macy, who he had come within months of marrying, didn't have the sincerity and zeal for life this Lexy seemed to possess. Macy was driven, but more towards climbing up the ladder of success than anything else. She had used the fiasco with Becky as an excuse to break up with him, but more than anything he thought it was his coaching career that bothered her the most. Lots of time and no money was not a formula for a successful match in her eyes.

Again, David thought of Lexy. She didn't know it, but he had watched her this past week. After their initial encounter, she had avoided him like the plague, and his brain told him to do the same, but he couldn't help himself. There was something about her which screamed for him to protect her and watch out for her. Her fierce independence actually reminded him of a bull pup. He had a feeling her tragic flaw was speaking before thinking. But he had to admit she had an amazing work ethic. She would come up to the school by 8 a.m. every morning ready to work to ensure the camp ran as smooth as possible. Sometimes, she didn't leave until 6 p.m., and he certainly didn't want to leave her on the campus alone. So he would find things to do until her jeep disappeared from the parking lot. Apparently, Camp Courage wasn't just a job to her; she really wanted to make the camp an experience to remember for the kids. He admired that, and that admiration is what walked him down to the cafeteria during the meeting.

He had full intention of showing up, signing a piece of paper, and then leaving. Then he heard her speech, and when she looked at him with eyes that swirled in brown, green, and gray, framed with lashes that seemed to go for miles, he knew he was getting himself into more than a volunteer position. He wanted the camp to not only be a success for the kids, but for her. He wondered how old she was; Jo said she was right out of college, so probably around twenty-two. At the ripe old age of twenty-eight and probably lots more life experience, he felt ancient next to her. He shook his head as he entered his office and dug out a file with the names and telephone numbers of his football players. *Stop, David. Do not go*

*down this road. She is here for six weeks.
Surely you can control yourself for six weeks.
She is a great big headache wrapped up in a
tiny little body and you should run, run far
away.* He was thinking all of those thoughts
as he looked at Monday on his calendar and
knew he couldn't wait to see her again.

Lexy got home around four that afternoon
and was met at the door with the scent of
baking apple pie. She shook her head. If she
didn't watch it she would be going on a
shopping spree for new clothes one size
larger than what she packed for the next six
weeks. Frannie was in the kitchen, donned
with an apron that said *God Bless the Cook*
across the chest. She was humming what
sounded like *Amazing Grace*. She looked up
as Lexy entered the kitchen.

"Hey, Lexy. How was your day?" She
was busy chopping onions, potatoes, and
carrots, gradually dumping handfuls in the
large crock-pot that contained what looked
like a simmering roast.

Lexy thought of her completed list as she
grabbed a carrot and started nibbling.
"Productive. My day was very productive."

Frannie smiled. "That's always a nice
feeling, isn't it?"

"Yes, it is."

Lexy heard the garage door open and close. Seconds later a very tired looking Jo came drudging up the steps. She attempted to smile at Lexy and Frannie, but her efforts failed. Frannie had stopped dinner preparations and stared at her. "What is it, Jo?"

Jo looked at Lexy, then her cousin. "We just had a rough day at the office, that's all. We're trying to get ready for the new school year and are short five math teachers, three English teachers, and ten special education teachers."

Lexy's mouth fell open. "Ten!"

"Yes."

Frannie looked from Jo to Lexy as she made Jo a much needed glass of iced tea. "Why the high turn over?"

Jo shrugged, gratefully accepted the refreshment and headed towards one of the cushioned kitchen chairs. She stretched and then laid her head on the table. "In a nutshell, the state and the nation are asking more than any one human being can give. Good teachers can be effective if they are allowed to be. With full inclusion and high stakes testing we're not allowing them to be. No one wants to commit themselves to a life of poverty just to get overworked and underappreciated."

Lexy listened to Jo's words that confirmed her worst fears. What if she too decided it wasn't for her? Was her education a total waste of four years? She didn't like thinking about it, but now couldn't help it.

Jo's regretful tone entered her thoughts. "Hey, Lexy. I'm sorry, honey. I didn't mean to be a cloud of discouragement. What will be will be. Just know if you ever decide to relocate to Augusta, there will be a job." She attempted a warm smile, but Lexy knew the day had taken its toll on Jo's enthusiasm for education. "Tell me about your day. How was your meeting?"

"It went really well. The volunteers are great. Nine women and one man showed up to fill the lead teacher positions and then I had ten volunteers; thirteen counting the music and art teachers, and then David."

Frannie dropped something in the kitchen and Jo placed a hand on Lexy's arm to interrupt her enthusiastic report. "Did you say David?"

"Yes….. David. David Griffin." Lexy was disturbed by the continuing glare of the two women. "Coach Griffin."

Jo laughed, a real laugh. "Well, well, well. Wonders never cease, do they Fran?"

Frannie was setting the table by this time, but Lexy didn't miss the raised eyebrow. "Nope, they do not."

Lexy looked between both women, thoroughly confused. "What? He said his brother, Tommy, was coming down the last two weeks. I'm sure he wants to spend time with him."

Jo was deep in thought as she munched on a baby carrot. "Did he only volunteer for the last two weeks?"

"No. He volunteered for the whole camp."

Frannie chimed in. "Is he getting paid?"

Lexy thought a minute. "Well, no. I mean we didn't talk about it. But I assumed he knew it was too late to turn in the paper work for paid positions."

Jo agreed. "Oh, I'm sure he knew about it. Being in an administrative position and all."

Lexy shrugged her shoulders. "So, what's the big deal?"

Jo thought a second. "Your brother is a coach, right?"

Lexy nodded.

"What are his summers like?"

"Hectic. Sara, his wife, is always complaining about how she never sees him. I guess he's trying to get ready for the fall."

"Right. So, do you think he would volunteer for a camp when he could be getting ready for the season?"

Lexy thought about Brad and his dedication to the sport. David seemed at least that dedicated, if not more. "No way."

Both women stared at her, as if waiting for her to process the information.

Lexy put her finger up in victory. "You know, it occurred to me this morning he wanted to keep an eye out for his territory, the gym you know, watch over to make sure nothing is out of place. I bet I was right." Lexy stopped. Something in her didn't want to believe that was it; she wanted to believe he wanted to be there, certainly not for her but for the kids. But maybe he did just want to watch what was his. Somehow, the thought didn't settle well in her spirit.

Jo gulped the last of her tea and stood up to go change before dinner. "You know what, Lexy? I bet you are right."

Lexy didn't see it, but Frannie stopped the preparation and stared at her cousin with an open mouth. Jo moved behind Lexy and quietly put her finger to her mouth and shook her head. Frannie nodded and continued humming *Amazing Grace*. And as Lexy retreated upstairs to change and get reorganized, she tried to decipher the overwhelming sense of disappointment dampening her spirit.

"Hi, baby."

A ray of warmth shot through Lexy's heart as she held the cell phone to her ear. "Hi, Mom."

A deeper voice entered the conversation. "Hi, little girl."

Lexy plopped on her bed, still smiling. "Hi, Daddy."

"How are you?" They said it at the same time and started laughing. It was so good to hear their voices the day before camp began. Just knowing they were there even if they were far away gave her reassurance.

"I'm fine. I miss you guys." Lexy cringed at the note of sadness in her voice; she was sure her parents picked up on it.

Her dad cleared his throat. "We miss you too, Alexandra."

She knew her mom was trying to be cheerful. "Are you ready for tomorrow, Lexy?"

"Yes m'am. I think so."

"Are you excited about meeting the kids?"

"Yeah, Daddy. I am. I can't wait to meet the faces behind the names I've been studying." She paused. "How's everything at home?"

"Oh the same as you left it. Brad is getting ready for football season. Sara is fine; keeping busy with teaching summer school. Billy called and is getting ready for a big community event. It is some type of festival the people look forward to every year."

"Have you heard from Brody?"

Silence…then her father finally spoke. "Yes. He makes sure he calls or comes over every couple of days to check on you. Do you hear from him a lot?"

She swallowed. The answer was yes and no. He called, and she had talked to him twice. But she didn't return the daily inquiry about her day's activities. And she got at least three text messages from him a day. It was proving to be too much for her, but she didn't want to get into that right now. "I've talked to him a couple of times….Hey guys?"

"Yes?"

"Pray for me, ok?"

Her dad spoke first. "How about we pray right now?"

Lexy closed her eyes, grateful for her parents and their faith. Soon the soothing tones of her father's voice requesting that God be with Lexy and the kids and the volunteers tomorrow and the duration of the camp set her heart at ease. He ended the prayer with thanksgiving, but also asking that God give Lexy discernment in all areas of her life. She wasn't sure what that last part meant, but she did know she slept like a baby and was eager to begin the job she had come to do.

Chapter 5

The registration tables were set up. *Check.*

Balloons were inflated and tied. *Check.*

All lead teachers were in place ready to receive each child as they came. *Check.*

Name tags were either being worn or ready to stick on. *Check.*

Go to the bathroom before 8 a.m. *Uh-Oh. No check! No check!*

Lexy threw her clipboard on the table as she walked fast (ok, jogged) towards the closest restroom. She was notorious for her ability to not go to the bathroom for hours despite her small stature, but when she had to go, well as her grandmother used to say, "Katy bar the door, because she's a coming!" But just as she saw the little welcoming stick figure of a lady pointing the way to relief, a wall appeared in front of her and knocked her to the ground. David.

At first all Lexy could do was close her eyes and pray silently, *Please, Lord. Don't let me wet my pants. Don't let me wet my pants.* David was leaning down offering a hand to help her up. She accepted, grateful she wasn't standing in a puddle.

"Lexy, I am so sorry. I didn't see you coming."

Lexy tried to stand still as he spoke, but she couldn't help it. The more he talked the more fidgety she became and soon she was swaying from side to side.

David was still talking. "I was looking for you. I wanted to ask you about some games I was thinking of playing….." He paused and cocked his head like a lost puppy dog. "Are you ok?"

"Well actually, no. I was on my way to go to the bathroom when we, well, you know. And I…."

David's eyes got big as he stepped out of the way. "Enough said…have at it. We'll talk later."

Lexy's run turned to a full blown sprint as she tossed thanks over her shoulder; she didn't see David stifling a chuckle as she retreated behind the concrete wall.

"Hey Lexy."

Lexy turned to meet the gaze of Karen Davis, a veteran teacher and camp counselor who had done this more than a few times. "Yes?"

She gave Lexy a thumbs up and mouthed, "Good Job."

Lexy smiled in gratitude. The morning had gone well. Seventy-five children showed up for registration and because of the efficiency of each volunteer, she got to talk to each of the parents and campers before the day began. There were many interesting encounters, one that was downright bizarre. At about 8:30 a.m., a little boy named Daniel arrived accompanied by what looked like his grandfather but turned out to be his father. The gentleman immediately sought out the director with Daniel in tow. When he reached Lexy the look on his face was obvious disbelief that standing in front of him was the woman who was supposed to control his son's behavior for six weeks.

"May I help you?" She inquired.

"Yes. Young lady, my name is Reverend Lewis and this is my son Daniel."

She held out her hand. Reverend Lewis ignored it and little Daniel, who appeared to be eight but was actually thirteen startled giggling uncontrollably. Lexy lowered her hand and got down on the boy's eye level. "Do you want to be here, Daniel?"

An expletive came out of his mouth that was meant to shock Lexy and get a reaction out of his father. It worked. The Reverend began to take his black leather belt off, but Lexy thought quick. Not wanting a scene on the first day she redirected Daniel to Coach Griffin who had rallied quite a few of the new arrivals and got them active in some games to take their minds off being left at camp. It seemed to be working. Daniel rambled off. She noticed his gate was awkward and his eyes wandered. Once Daniel was off and running, Lexy looked at Mr. Lewis and reassured him they would do their best to make Daniel feel at home.

He was putting his belt back in place and responded in a fire and brimstone kind of voice. "He's a rough one, that one. Don't really know where he came from. But you have got to watch him. You'll regret it if you don't."

Reverend Lewis turned to leave and Lexy felt the hairs raise up on her arms. Laura Mason came over and gave her a one armed hug. "I know Daniel. He goes to my school. His dad is right. He can rewire this entire school in a matter of minutes. We do have to keep a close eye on him. But don't worry. Little Daniel can't throw anything at us we can't handle."

Lexy threw a brief prayer up to heaven asking that Laura be right.

Besides Daniel's introduction, everything else went smoothly. Every group had gathered in the cafeteria ready for the center time rotations to begin. Lexy thought about the system she had put in place; the whole camp had taken on a sports motif, with each group being named after a college football team. The center rotation consisting of art, music, reading time, and cooking was posted in the cafeteria, as well as inside each team leader and volunteer's notebook. At precisely 9:15 a.m., rotations began and continued until 12:15, when each of the groups would gather for lunch and medication distribution. Then at 12:45 p.m. the groups would get ready for one final split center where half the children would stay in the cafeteria for free dance time and the other half would go to the gym for a planned activity with David. At 1:45 p.m., the groups reconvened and got ready to go home for the day. This schedule would be in place except for when a group outing was planned, and this week the adventure was to the indoor swimming pool on Wednesday. Lexy still needed to work out the details for that outing, but for now she would concentrate on the day at hand. Lexy looked at each group and her heart warmed. The preschoolers, led by Mrs. Davis, proudly held the name of the Georgia Bulldogs, or Pups in this case. All of the other groups were intermingled, with signs above their table that read Gators, Volunteers, Crimson Tide, Razorbacks, Tigers, Wildcats, Rebels, Gamecocks, and

Commodores. The teachers and volunteers wore the team colors. One of the younger volunteers, Kacy Jones, had helped Lexy make arm bands that identified each child by their name and group. Lexy blew her whistle to get the attention of the campers and volunteers. It worked because everyone stopped talking and stared at her. All 98 faces.

Lexy cleared her throat. "Good morning." She waited. After a second, everyone caught on and responded. "Good morning."

"My name is Lexy. Welcome to Camp Courage. In a few moments we will begin center time. Two groups will go to each center and we will rotate every 45 minutes. "Are you ready to have some fun?"

"Yes!"

"Ok." She blew her whistle. "Go!"

And off they went.

By 10:45 a.m., two rotations had occurred with no problems. Lexy was beginning to think her days were going to be too easy. Then a reality check in the form of an eight year little boy old named Noah claimed her attention. His counselor, a fairly new teacher by the name of Maria, walked with him down to the office. They came through the door and poor Maria looked like she was going to either break down and cry or bust out laughing.

Lexy tried to be as encouraging as possible. "Hi, Maria. Hi, Noah."

Maria looked down at Noah who was not looking at either of them. Instead he had dropped to all fours and began to bark like a dog. Lexy raised her eyebrows.

Maria whispered. "He's been doing this since we rotated into art class."

Lexy stared a moment before processing the situation. Then, something that she didn't know she had kicked in.

"Hmmm. Well, Mr. Noah. Let's see what we can find out about barking, scratching and sniffing."

She stepped behind the counter and grabbed a file marked *behavior plans*. She pulled Noah's and scanned it. "Aha." She read the typed comments of the previous teacher. *Noah has difficulty transitioning from one activity to another.* She watched as Noah attempted to sniff in the corner of the office and agreed wholeheartedly. She continued reading. *Holding his hand when walking from one activity to the next helps signal change. It also prevents him from escapist behavior.* Lexy heard the escapist growling as Maria edged closer to the door. *Lord, help me with this one.* She reached in her desk and grabbed a handful of something before turning to the teacher. "Maria, I'll talk to Noah and bring him down when he is ready, Ok?"

Maria looked like she was ready to kiss her as she walked out the heavy wooden door.

Lexy sat in one of the chairs meant for visitors to the office. "Hmmm, well Noah. We have to figure this out buddy." He continued jumping around on all fours. Lexy didn't try to stop him, but continued talking.

"If you can't participate at camp, then maybe we need to call dad from work to come get you."

Noah slowed down a bit.

"You know, I met your dad this morning. He seemed very nice."

The barking stopped.

"In fact, he told me if you gave us any trouble to call him at work."

One big blue eye looked at Lexy from underneath the long blonde bowl cut.

She smiled. "So, what do you think? Should we call dad to come get you?"

Noah was apparently thinking.

"Of course, he also mentioned that he would put you to work pulling weeds and doing some yard work outside of his office— just to keep you busy. I don't know about you, but I don't like yard work much. I'd much rather be at camp."

Noah was sitting back on his knees, both eyes on hers.

"Do you want to stay at camp, Noah?"

Noah nodded his head vigorously.

Lexy leaned forward to make eye contact. She spoke in a hushed whisper, "Ok, let's make a deal then. When it is time to rotate centers, I want you to find a teacher and hold their hand. They will walk you to the next center and be your buddy until you feel like everything will be ok. If you get really uncomfortable I want you to hand your teachers one of these."

She handed him three red tokens. He held them in the palm of his hands and looked up at her with those big blue eyes. He really was a beautiful child; Lexy couldn't help but wonder about his diagnosis.

"If you give your teachers one of these, they will know you need a break. Then you can come see me. But if you keep your three tokens all day, you can come to me at the end of camp and trade them in for a treat."

A hint of a smile crossed the little guy's face.

"Deal?"

He nodded his head.

"Can you use your words, Noah?"

The softest sound came out of his mouth, but it was definitely a yes.

"Ok, let's walk you back to class."

She held her hand out to him and he took it without hesitation.

David held his breath the whole time while he watched from across the office. He was on the other side of the wall facing Lexy so she didn't see him, but he saw her. He watched the tender interaction and had to remind himself she had never actually stepped foot in a classroom before. She was truly a natural with these kids, and he couldn't help but be mesmerized by her gentle voice and non-intimidating approach. After he was sure she had gone, he scribbled a note on a pad and left it where he knew she would see it. He wasn't sure why he did it, but he knew his admiration for Lexy was growing by the second.

Lexy reentered the front office getting the medication ready for distribution. She glanced down and saw a handwritten note that was not there before she walked Noah down to class. It was in red pen and looked like it was scribbled by a man in a hurry. It simply read, *I like your style. -- David*.

    She reread the note and wandered what he was referring to. Had he seen her in the office with Noah? Whatever it was, the fact that David Griffin liked her style did strange things to her insides. Her heart flip flopped and she got the feeling she always did when she aced a test or won a tennis match. What was this about? She looked down at the large medication box and chart. She couldn't think about it right now, but soon she would know exactly what David liked about her style.

Chapter 6

The remainder of the first day of camp flew by. Most activities went smoothly for the exception of a couple of minor glitches. But now, parents had arrived and all of the children had gone home. The teachers and volunteers were packing up, and Lexy made sure she took time to encourage and thank each one of them. After spending a few minutes with Laura Mason, who could potentially be a very good friend, Lexy headed towards the gym to find David. She wanted to thank him as well. She had seen him during the first afternoon rotation and was amazed at his ability to manage such a large, diverse group of children with enough finesse to make him look like a pro. He had games prepared and had even recruited some of his football players to help during the afternoon sessions. They were great and Lexy could tell they held their coach in high esteem. She had to admit regardless of their beginnings, David Griffin was a pretty nice guy.

Lexy entered the gym, finding David alone cleaning up the various centers. He didn't look up, but casually commented. "To be so little you walk like a herd of elephants." He paused before looking up. "Or like a woman on a mission. How was the first day?"

The butterflies slumbering in her stomach woke up and began to play. He was walking towards her holding a basketball, smiling. Lexy was having a hard time concentrating, the closer he got. She looked down at the ground, examining her pink toenails. Something was wrong with her; she had never been one to go gaga over the opposite sex. Granted, she had her share of crushes, and she could appreciate a good looking man, but this was ridiculous. Brody was a "hottie", as some of her friends had told her in the past. His boyish good looks had more than one girl on campus envying her. But David, well David was a man, one that exuded confidence, borderline arrogance, but also compassion and mercy. *Good grief Lexy. Get a grip.* She looked up as he reached her. The smile on his face reached up to his eyes and it almost took her breath away. It was her turn to talk.

She stuttered. "It was good. Really good. With the exception of a couple of camper meltdowns, it ran pretty smoothly."

"Yeah, I witnessed one of those meltdowns."

She raised her eyebrows. "Is that what you meant in the note?"

"Yep. Nice work, Teach." He was dribbling the ball back and forth as he maintained eye contact with her.

No one had ever called her Teach. She liked it. "Thanks. Noah managed to walk on two legs for the rest of the day."

David laughed, but said nothing. He just looked at her. It was unnerving.

She was determined to hold his gaze, despite her nerves. "Thanks for today, David. I appreciate all your hard work. It means a lot."

"You are welcome." More staring.

She cleared her throat and turned to go. "Well, have a good afternoon."

"Hey, Lexy?"

She turned as he passed her the basketball. "Do you shoot as good as you throw?"

Oh no. A challenge. This could be dangerous. She raised her brows and smirked, passing the ball back to him. "Yeah. Actually, I do."

He slowly nodded his head towards the basket. "Wanna play some one on one?"

A slow smile spread across her face. She held up one foot. "I don't think I can hold my own in my flip flops."

David shrugged his shoulders and kicked off his shoes. "We'll play barefoot."

She couldn't help but giggle. "Really?"

"Really."

She kicked off her shoes. "Ok. First one to 21 wins."

"Deal."

Thirty minutes later, David looked across the court at Lexy and was amazed at how such a small package could pack such a punch. They were tied 20-20 and she had the ball. He ran to guard her and block her shot but she was quick, turned and ran up to score a lay up. 21, she won. She was jumping up and down in celebration, her walking shorts and T shirt soaked in sweat and her dark curly hair matted in ringlets stuck to her face. Her face was flushed and her eye makeup had started to run. She was the most beautiful thing he had ever seen. He leaned over to catch his breath, but not from running.

He looked up to see her walking towards her flip flops. She threw a concerned tone of mock concern over her shoulder. "You ok, David?"

He shook his head, trying to shrug off the effect she had on him. "Yeah, I'll make it. Where did you learn to play like that?"

Lexy looked at him, clearly amused. "I have a sports crazy dad and two older brothers. They taught me everything I know."

"Then you're not the only good teacher in the family."

She shrugged her shoulders. "Guess not....thanks."

"So what else do you play?"

Lexy was walking towards him with the basketball. "Flag football, basketball, softball, tennis, track…You name it, I play it." She hesitated. "Except for golf."

"Golf?"

"Yeah, don't like golf."

"Why?"

"Too long, too much work, not enough pay off for putting the ball in the hole."

He narrowed his eyes at her. "Could it be that you are not any good at golf?"

She bit her bottom lip and crinkled her nose. "Could be."

David laughed. "Competitive, aren't we?"

"Yes." Lexy looked down, apparently embarrassed. "Well, David thanks for the game. It was fun." She smiled mischievously and held out her hand. "No hard feelings?"

David took her hand, noticing how it fit in his. "Never."

She passed him the ball and whispered. "Have a good afternoon."

He nodded.

She turned to go and had almost reached the double doors when he called out to her. She turned and he was right behind her. Lexy raised her eyebrows, surprised by his nearness. "Yes?"

"I have a proposition for you."

She cocked one eyebrow and waited.

"I need someone to work out with in the mornings. You know, cardio, weights, occasional one on one…"

"And?"

"Do you want to meet me up here at 7:00 a.m. and work out?"

She hesitated but he hurriedly continued. "We would be finished in time for you to get ready for camp. The girl's locker room has showers, so you could clean up and change beforehand."

She cherished her morning jogs and had always reveled in the alone time. But now, the idea of meeting David in the morning didn't seem like an invasion, but more the chance to make a new friend. She liked it.

"Ok."

He looked surprised. "Ok?"

She smiled and nodded her head. "I'll see you at 7."

"Great." He turned to jog off. She opened one of the doors to leave, but again he stopped her, this time with his coaching voice. "Don't be late."

She put her hands on her hips and stared at him. "I'm never late, David."

He laughed. "See you tomorrow."

She was late.

It was 6:56 a.m. and she was just pulling out of Jo and Frannie's driveway. She slept through her alarm after a late night talking to her mom and dad, then Brody on the phone. The conversation with her parents was encouraging. She still missed them, but was also having a lot of fun spreading her wings, so to speak. The conversation with Brody was much more painful. Lexy could not remember a time when she felt more uncomfortable talking with someone she cared for; he was miserable and said so. She wasn't and said so. He wanted to come visit. She said no. He asked why. She couldn't come up with a reason. He got angry. She thought it was time to take a break. He didn't. They hung up. Nothing was resolved. She couldn't sleep, feeling like her insides were in turmoil, but not necessarily over Brody. She prayed that God would give her peace to know what to do in that situation. Jeremiah 29:11 came to mind and it comforted her, it was just that sometimes she wished she knew the plans God had for her, too. Glancing at the speedometer told her she was driving too fast, but she desperately did not want to be late. At 7:02 a.m., she pulled into the school parking lot. David was stretching by his old pickup truck, but he looked up with a jerk of his head when she screeched into the space beside him. The look on his face did not speak of good mornings. Lexy frowned. Apparently, he really was mad that she was late.

He crossed his arms over his chest and watched her dismount from the jeep. Well, late or not she was in no mood to be scolded. "Sorry I'm late."

No words. Just staring. *Come on, David. Words, words!*

She grabbed her gym bag from the back and faced him. "Look David, its only two minutes. I'm sorry…."

His look and tense body language softened, a little bit anyway. "Is that why you were driving like a maniac? Because you didn't want to be late?"

"Well, yeah."

He moved his arms from across his chest and placed both hands on her shoulders. His gentle touch was sending tingles all over her body, making it nearly impossible for her to concentrate. But apparently he had something to say. He moved closer and looked down into her eyes. "Lex, I was just teasing about being late. Please don't ever drive like that again. It's dangerous when you rush like that. I don't want you in an accident, especially when you are trying to prove something to me. Promise me you won't do that again."

Lexy looked around. Had her mother driven up from Jacksonville and taken the form of the gentle giant who was definitely giving her a lecture, one she had heard about six dozen times from her own mom? He placed his index finger under her chin and directed her gaze back towards him. "Promise?"

She tried not to laugh; he was sweet to be concerned. Lexy wasn't sure if she liked the idea of him thinking she was trying to please him. That wasn't it; was it? Afterall, why should she care what he thought? It was just that the look in his eyes that moment was one of such concern, she couldn't help but respond in a gentle voice. "I'll be more careful, David. I promise."

He stepped back half a step and gave her a little more space. "Ok. Now let's warm up with a jog and then I thought we would lift weights and end with a little one on one. Ready?"

She laughed, enjoying the closeness of him. "All that in an hour?"

He nodded his head and she noticed the way his jaw was set when his determination came to the surface. "Yep."

"Lead the way."

"Put your bag back in the jeep and we'll pick it up on the way in. I thought we could jog the trail around the school."

"That sounds good."

They both started jogging and fell into an easy pace. After several minutes, they found their rhythm and just enjoyed the scenery. The school was nestled in some pretty woods and Lexy really enjoyed the peacefulness of it all. David didn't feel the need to talk, and Lexy appreciated it.

Less than an hour later, they finished up with a short game of HORSE. This time, David won and Lexy couldn't help but let her competitive spirit get the better of her when she lightly shoved him across the court. It really wasn't her fault that he tripped and fell on his butt in the process of her slight tantrum. Apparently all was forgiven when David led her to the girl's locker room, laughing; Lexy found that the once familiar setting of a locker room brought back a ton of memories from her days playing high school and college sports. But Lexy wasn't dwelling on the past; instead her mind was on the present and the good time she had working out and laughing with a very different kind of friend.

In less than thirty minutes she was ready. She looked at her watch. 8:30 a.m. She still had a few minutes to do a devotional. All she had to do was find a quiet place. After grabbing her Bible and journal from her bag, she decided to go to the stadium and sit on one of the bleachers. She stood on the top bleacher searching for a nice place to sit. Out of the corner of her eye she saw another figure settled down with what looked like a book and paper. He had his back to her, with his head down, obviously praying. She wouldn't interrupt. Instead, she turned around and decided to let David have his quiet time in peace.

His words were softly spoken, barely audible. "Lord, I don't know why you sent her into my life. I know I'm not perfect. I fail in living for you every single day, but God I thought I was here for a reason. I thought you wanted me to witness to these boys and build a program that was an example of You to the community. We've gone through trials and You have been faithful in them all. But now, I'm distracted by her. I'm drawn to just about everything about her. She drives me crazy and scares me to death and makes me laugh. But God I don't want my heart walking around in the form of a 5'3'' pack of dynamite who doesn't know when to quit and pushes herself entirely too hard. I'm scared. Give we wisdom, God."

He listened. After several moments a verse from long ago came to mind. Proverbs 3:5. *Trust in the Lord with all your heart and lean not on your own understanding; in all your ways acknowledge him, and he will make your paths straight.*

David nodded his head with his eyes still closed. "I'll trust You Lord. You're right. I don't understand it, but You are in charge of me, God. Guide me in Your will. –And protect me from wanting to put duct tape over her mouth. In Jesus' name. Amen"

David took a deep breath, stood up and stretched, readying himself for a new day.

Chapter 7

Lexy could hardly believe it, but she was quickly approaching the last two weeks of camp. Overall it had been an interesting four weeks. Initially, they had to overcome quite a few obstacles like getting to know each camper and his or her specific medical needs. There were some bathroom fiascos that turned into water wars; the day at the pool was enlightening between changing all of the campers into their swimsuits and figuring out who could actually swim. Little Daniel Lewis decided it would be funny to pull the fire alarm, thus causing a complete evacuation thirty minutes ahead of time. But, they all survived unscathed and for that Lexy was grateful. There was the hay ride at the petting zoo, where little Pam who everyone affectionately called spider monkey because she could scale you in a matter of seconds, got a little on edge because of an overly friendly pony and climbed David like a monkey on a tree. Lexy would have paid about a million dollars to have a picture of David's expression as the beautiful little china doll of a girl with her jet black hair camped on top of his head.

It was 2:15 p.m. and all of the teachers and volunteers had gathered in the cafeteria for the weekly report. Lexy looked at all the people who had become her friends and once again, thanked them all, gave them an updated list of campers for next week, and wished them a great weekend. She was gathering her stuff together when the only male teacher, Joel Simpson, approached her. She liked Joel. He was always positive with the kids and very agreeable to any change of plans. Lexy was beginning to learn flexibility was a huge asset when working with children with special needs.

"Hi, Joel. What's up?" His brown eyes and light brown curly hair, coupled with his friendly demeanor reminded her of Kirk Cameron.

"Lexy, I was wondering if you would be interested in having dinner with me tonight?"

Lexy was glad her hands were not full because she was sure she would have dropped whatever she was holding. Never in a million years had she expected this; she assumed Joel was married with children. And even though he was nice, there was no attraction there whatsoever. Lexy realized the moments passing were making the situation more awkward.

Joel stammered on. "Look, I understand if you don't. The rumor is you and David have something going on, and I…."

"Excuse me?"

Joel's eyes got big at her tone. "Well, people have said you two meet in the mornings and, well, and…"

She snapped a little bit. "Work out in the gym, and then we go our separate ways."

His face was an interesting shade of red. "Lexy, I didn't mean to offend…"

She felt bad for sounding so rude. Her voice softened. "Joel, actually I was involved with someone before I left Jacksonville and I'm not ready to pursue anything else, especially since I'm only here for a couple more weeks. I'm flattered you asked, really. But you can do me a favor and tell anyone that mentions it that David and I are not going out."

Joel nodded his head and smiled sheepishly. "You can't blame a guy for trying, right?"

"Right. Like I said I'm flattered."

He gave her a friendly hug and left the cafeteria. Lexy gathered her stuff and walked down to the office. She was sure her face was red just thinking about people talking about her and David. Maybe she should stop meeting him. Just the thought of it saddened her. These last few weeks had been the beginning of a great friendship. She really liked David Griffin as a person. He was fun and full of spirit and competitiveness, but also had a strong faith about him. He still didn't know she discovered the place he prayed and read his bible. But everyday, after they were finished, he went out there for at least thirty minutes. She admired his priorities, and the last thing David needed was talk about them in the community, especially after the unfortunate incident with Becky. As if her thoughts summoned him, she heard his voice behind her.

"What are you so focused on?"

She turned to face him and he was smiling. He must have showered and changed because he looked clean and disarmingly handsome in his red pull-over and khaki shorts. His hair was freshly combed; in fact this might be the first time she had seen him without his CHS baseball cap. His hair was dark and curly, almost black; it wasn't long, but it wasn't cropped short to his head either. The contrast of his hair with his bright green eyes was amazing. David was also wearing some kind of cologne that consumed everyone of her senses, including speech.

"Lexy? Are you ok?" He moved forward and touched her arm.

Not helping! She tried to respond, but no words came out. *Come on girl, speak. You can do it.*

She moved one step back attempting to disconnect the electrical flow coursing through her veins. "I'm ok, just um, well you will never believe what happened after my meeting a few minutes ago."

True to form he didn't respond, just leaned back on the desk, crossed his long, tan, rather hairy legs and waited.

"Joel asked me out."

His jaw tightened. "Hmmm. What did you say?"

"I told him no."

His jaw relaxed. "Is that all?"

She shook her head. "No. He asked me if I turned him down because of you."

No words, just eyebrows.

She put her hands on her hips and tried to laugh it off. "Can you believe that?"

His voice stayed even. "What did you tell him?"

"I told him we weren't a couple. Just friends."

"Oh." There was something in his voice that indicated disappointment, or was she just imagining things? "Was that it?"

Mr. Man of Few Words was starting to get on her nerves. "What do you mean?"

"Did he ask for a reason other than us?"

She thought about it; Joel hadn't asked, she had volunteered the information. "No. But I told him I had just gotten out of a relationship with my boyfriend and didn't want to pursue anything else, especially since I'm only here for a couple more weeks."

He didn't move, except for the jaw tightening again. Finally, he spoke. "Was that the truth?"

Lexy shrugged her shoulders. "Well, yeah. I did just break up with my boyfriend. Sorta-I mean I told him we should take a break. He said no. We hung up. Nothing was really resolved. I haven't talked to him since, but I am only here for a couple more weeks."

"Is that the only reason you said no to Joel?"

Now she leaned back on the counter and folded her arms. Her tone told of her aggravation. "Do you think I should go out with Joel?"

He smirked. *Irritating.*

"Do you want to?"

She huffed. "No."

"Why not?"

She combed her fingers through her hair. "I just told you."

"Is that it?"

116

Her voice went up a notch. "What do you want me to say?"

"I want you to tell me the truth."

"Joel is not my type."

"Why didn't you tell him that?"

"Because that would have been rude."

"But truthful."

"There is such a thing as tact, David."

"Alexandra, I have seen you without tact before, remember?"

Low blow. And he used her full name, which was reserved only for her father. She was about ready to show him a little less tact when he got up from his leaning position and moved two steps closer to her. If she started to sway from the intoxication of that scent and some kind of very masculine soap, it would be embarrassing. Nevertheless, she looked fully into his face and decided to challenge him a bit. "Aren't you upset about people talking about us going out?"

He looked into her eyes, which forced her to hold his gaze. *Ok, Lexy, get a grip. True, his eyes do look like some kind of rare jewel. And his mouth, well his mouth happened to be perfect. It was moving, saying something. What was he saying?* "Why would I be upset about that?"

"Because, because…" *Oh no.* He didn't know she knew about any of the other stuff. What was she going to say?

"Because of Becky?"

She nodded her head.

He didn't look mad, but almost relieved. "Jo told you?"

She whispered. "Yes."

He sat down in the swivel chair in front of her, which put him just below eye level. "Lexy, that situation taught me, or rather God taught me through that situation to focus on the truth, and to dismiss what is not true. Now you and I are not going out. That is the truth."

"Right. End of story." She turned around in order to pretend to be busy with something rather than have him see the unexplainable sting in her eyes. But his blasted hand stopped her and she turned to him.

"So, do you want to go get some dinner with me tonight?"

Her mother always told her that hanging your mouth open in surprise was not attractive, but she guessed she forgot in this situation because a whole family of flies could have flown in. "What?"

He stood up and laughed. Again, he was hovering. David's eyes were dancing as he brushed a stray hair off her face. "Is your

118

brain fried from this week? Dinner, tonight, with me. What do you say?"

"I, David…" She shook her head and looked down at the worn carpet.

"Is that a no?"

When she looked up, he was smirking. "It's not a no, it's just, well…"

"Am *I* not your type?" He was obviously teasing her and it was more than a little irritating.

Now what was she supposed to say to that? She didn't even really know what her type was, did she? She put her hands on her hips and tried to finish a sentence. "David…"

He bent down and tweaked her nose. "What? Are you afraid?"

She stomped her foot. "Quit cutting me off!" He actually smiled at her outburst. *Infuriating.*

"Come on, Alexandra. Be a grown up. Do you like me or not?"

Oh, now it was on. She placed both hands on his chest and pushed him—a little bit. "Excuse me? Grow up? Did you just tell me to grow up?"

He fell into the chair, but was smiling like he had won a fight. "Dinner?"

Before she could stop herself, she stomped her foot like a two year old and accepted the invitation. He wheeled towards her, stood up, and kissed her on the head. "I'll pick you up at Jo's. Be ready at 7." Then, he walked out of the office. She could have sworn she heard him laughing.

Lexy's head was pounding by the time she climbed the stairs to her loft. Why had she accepted that dinner invitation? He basically bullied her into saying yes; something she realized after the fact. She looked at her watch…4:00 p.m. Three hours until he came to pick her up. What was she going to tell Jo and Frannie? Where were they, anyway? They were usually home by this time, ready to feed her and hear about her day. She had come to love both of them like her own family. In fact, spoiled was probably a good word to describe her after four weeks of living with them. Nevertheless, she had grown through conversation, prayers, and observations. Her parents' wisdom was a blessing. She did need to spread her wings, and here, she felt like she was soaring. But now this. She hadn't really even tied up loose ends with Brody. Was this even right? The last time she talked to her parents, they said they had seen Brody at a Jacksonville University Summer kickoff, and he acted as if nothing had changed. But truthfully, things had changed on her part. She wasn't in love with anyone, or at least she didn't think so. Regardless, she knew she wasn't in love with Brody. It wasn't right to maintain a relationship when she didn't return his feelings.

And there was no use in starting something she couldn't finish. She knew herself well enough to know that David affected her in every possible way. His presence in a room lit up her eyes, but also made her uncomfortable. His voice was calming, yet could set her on edge in a skinny minute.

She flopped on her bed and looked over at her closet. She sat up with a start. What in the world was she going to wear? She had shorts, tank tops, a couple of pairs of capris, a few blouses and a bathing suit. She did have a couple of dresses for church but those seemed too dressy for dinner. She didn't have time to go shopping…maybe shorts would be ok, he didn't say dress up, but…oh her head was pounding. She walked to the bathroom, popped a couple of Aleve, and said a prayer that Jesus would return before 7:00 p.m.

Lexy had no more said amen when a knock on the door interrupted her thoughts.

"Come in."

Jo and Frannie came walking in giggling, loaded up with shopping bags.

Lexy enjoyed their playfulness, even if her mood and head didn't agree. "And just where have you two been?"

They responded in unison. "Shopping."

Lexy swept the abundance of bags with her hands. "Obviously."

She sat, legs crossed like an eager child, on her bed and bounced up and down, excited about their purchases despite her throbbing head. "Show me the goods."

Jo laughed. "We thought you would never ask."

The first outfit she pulled out was a gorgeous powder blue pant suit from Ann Taylor, one of Lexy's favorite stores. It was stunning, and apparently they had completed the outfit with a champagne colored cami, peak toe heels, and a simple irredescent pendant and matching earrings. "Wow! Jo you are going to knock them dead in that."

Jo looked at Lexy and playfully rolled her eyes. "Girl, which leg do you think I could fit in that suit? It's not for me."

Fran chimed in, "And don't look at me! I haven't seen that size since birth…"

Finally, it dawned on her. They had gone shopping for her. Lexy could feel the emotion flood her eyes and throat. She reached out to touch the suit. It felt wonderful. "Why?"

They sat on either side of her, both giving her a one armed hug. Frannie spoke. "Because we love you and want you to have a nice suit to wear for a job interview whenever the time comes."

Lexy cleared her throat. "Thank you." She looked at both of them. "I can't wait to wear it."

"Good. But that's not all." Lexy stared at Fran wide-eyed. Fran held up her bag from another one of her favorite stores. "We couldn't just get you something for work—as young as pretty as you are, you need something fun too." Lexy watched as Fran brought out a simple black linen dress with spaghetti straps, adorable black sandals, and another set of matching necklace and earrings, along with an elegant black clutch. It was perfect for her. It was perfect for tonight.

Lexy shook her head. "You guys are too much. You didn't have to…"

Jo stopped her. "Don't say it. I hate it when people say that. Of course, we didn't. We wanted to." She reached over and patted her knee.

"How did you know what size?"

Jo didn't hesitate. "Fran snooped through your closet." Jo ducked as Fran swung her pocketbook and hit Jo in the head.

Jo held up her hands to block the blow. "Ow."

"You're too old to lie." Fran looked at Lexy. "I folded some of your laundry the other day and peaked at the tag. I hope you don't mind."

Lexy smiled and hugged them again. "I don't mind. Thanks. In fact, you guys solved a problem I was trying to figure out."

Jo was hanging the suit and dress on the door of the closet. "Oh, really?"

Lexy knew her announcement would warrant a reaction, so she tried to brace herself. "I'm going out to dinner tonight."

Both women snapped their heads towards Lexy so quickly, she was afraid they were going to need icepacks later. She continued. "Yes." She looked down at her fingernails. "With David Griffin."

The ladies apparently hadn't heard Elizabeth King's fly catcher lecture because their open mouths were announcing vacancies. Finally, Frannie spoke and very nearly jumped up from the bed. "Well, it's about time!"

Jo smiled. "I'll say."

Lexy shook her head in confusion. "I don't get it, guys. I'm only here for a couple more weeks. I don't know what good can come from this."

Jo sat on the bed again, looking at Lexy with a strange expression. "Do you like him?"

Lexy nodded her head, but then threw her hands up in the air. "Yes, but he drives me insane half the time. He is arrogant and competitive and bossy. He's too big…."

Frannie threw her head back and fell on the bed laughing like a teenager.

Jo glanced behind her and shook her head. Lexy continued. "Well, he is."

"Then why did you say yes?" Jo wondered out loud.

"Because he tricked me."

Frannie sat up. "Tricked you?"

Jo disagreed in her assistant superintendent voice. "You're too smart to be tricked, young lady."

Lexy knew that and said so.

The room got quiet. Frannie jumped up with an idea. "Lexy, it is almost 5:00. This is what I want you to do. Come downstairs and have a snack….

Lexy playfully rolled her eyes. "Frannie…"

"Tut..tut..No arguing. Snack, then nap, then shower, then fashion show. Then you will be ready to go when David comes to pick you up."

At this point, Lexy was too overwhelmed and too tired to think about it anymore.

Jo chimed in. "Actually, I think that is a fabulous idea." She slapped Lexy on the knee before grabbing her arm and helping her off the bed. "Come on, kiddo. Time to eat."

Lexy looked at the beautiful clothes and shook her head. "You should have bought a bigger size."

Jo smiled knowingly. "Nope. I think they are just right."

Wise women are gifts from above. Lexy remembered reading that somewhere, and after a snack, nap, and a shower, the headache had disappeared and so had some of the angst about tonight, so she had to agree. She had already modeled the suit ensemble for the ladies downstairs and they loved it, as did she. It was a perfect fit; Lexy could see herself going to a job interview and feeling very confident. Next, was the black dress for tonight. She looked at her watch. It was 6:45 p.m. Fifteen minutes until she faced her giant. Before she had a chance to reach for the dress hanging on the closet door she saw headlights, but they weren't those of David's pickup. Instead a very nice red sports car pulled up and out came….David. Lexy bit her bottom lip because the sight of the car was nothing compared to the sight of the man. He was dressed in dark washed jeans and a sport coat over a white shirt, open at the neck. From her distance above he was gorgeous; she prayed she didn't make a fool of herself once they were breathing the same air.

Well here he was. In Jo's driveway. To pick up Lexy. He had prayed about this for a month and all God's wisdom pointed to one truth. He loved her. He didn't want to and wasn't willing to admit it for a long time, but God knocked on his heart until he opened it up and saw her face—everywhere he went. Now the horrible events with Becky and Macy made sense. God used it for good. Macy wasn't meant to be his because he never felt for her what he felt for Lexy. True, Lexy was obstinate, foolish, and proud sometimes but so was he. He reached the top of the steps and knocked on the door.

Frannie's face, wearing a mischievous smile, appeared. He rolled his eyes, waiting for an invitation, but she crossed her arms and didn't move.

Jo suddenly appeared. "Well, well, Fran. Wonders never cease. We haven't seen this guy for, hmmmm, let me see…six weeks, is it?"

Fran nodded her head. "Yep. It was about the time our young room mate moved in. Coincidence, huh?"

Jo tweaked his arm. "I think not."

David laughed while grabbing his arm. "Are you two going to let me in or harass me all night?"

Frannie reached up and patted his face— hard. "It's about time, you big lug!"

David rubbed his face. "Ow!"

Jo followed up with a hug and let him know all was apparently forgiven, but he had a strange feeling the inquisition had not begun yet. Finally, they invited him in. Frannie fixed him a glass of his favorite drink, half lemonade, half unsweet tea. "Thanks, Fran."

"You're welcome."

They all sat and he looked around. "Where is she?"

"Getting ready." Jo winked. "She'll be down soon enough. In the meantime, what are your intentions with our Lexy?"

David almost spit his drink across the room. "You're Lexy?"

Fran nodded her head and threw a pillow in his direction. He huffed at the abuse.

"Yes. She's as dear to us as our own children."

He looked at Jo and narrowed his eyes. "Do you like her more than me?"

She smiled, knowing he was half serious. "Sometimes. Sometimes I like you better. You're both bull headed and need your butt kicked once in a while."

David looked down at his feet before making eye contact. "Yeah, I know."

"You willing to do that?"

David noted and respected Jo's serious expression. He knew what she meant. "Yeah, I am. And she can kick mine back. I love her Jo." He watched his tough assistant superintendent/surrogate mother tear up. Fran grabbed two tissues, one for her and one for her cousin. About that time, Lexy's familiar elephant walk came bounding down the stairs. They heard the door open and close. She rounded the corner with a shy smile and David immediately stood up almost knocking his drink to the floor. He wasn't known for his abundant use of words, but it had never been because he didn't have them, except for now. He was speechless.

The woman standing in front of him looked very different from the tomboy he saw during the week. Her long curly hair was cascading down her back, framing her face. She didn't wear much makeup, but those hazel eyes were shining. The dress fit her like a glove, showing off her athletic build and great tan. He couldn't take his eyes off the sprinkle of freckles across her nose and shoulders. She was beautiful and she was still waiting for him to speak.

"Hi, David."

He moved closer, afraid she might change her mind and not go through with the date if he moved too fast. He whispered. "Hi." Time seemed to stand still as he tried to take her in.

Jo and Frannie cleared their throats. Jo broke the spell. "Lexy, you look stunning. That dress is enchanting."

Frannie agreed. "Yes, it is. Don't you think so, David?"

He heard his name and it brought his attention to the two other women in the room. "Excuse me?"

Frannie bit her bottom lip, trying not to smile. "I was just saying how Lexy looks…"

He finished Fran's sentence with his own adjective. "perfect."

Lexy began to turn red. She grabbed her new black clutch and kissed Jo and Fran goodbye. David took her hand, hugged both women and headed to the car. It was then that Lexy commented on his mode of transportation. She stood back and admired it openly. "Well, well, well…a red mustang? What happened to the pickup?"

"I take the pickup to school in case the boys or any of my students get a little mischievous. The mustang stays at home."

"Smart man."

He was moving to the passenger side. She followed. He opened the door and she slid in comfortably. The dark grey leather smelled new and the interior was spotless. David got in on the other side and buckled his seatbelt. He reached for the CD changer. "What kind of music do you like?"

"Anything's ok."

He looked at her with a strange expression. "So if I brought out some hard core rock, you wouldn't mind?"

She turned so she could see him. He was challenging her and she knew it. "Is that the kind of music you like?"

"No. But I asked you for a reason." His voice softened. "I want to know things like that about you, Lexy. I'm really interested."

She took a deep breath and turned her head to stare out the front windshield. "Casting Crowns, Avalon, Third Day, The David Crowder Band, Jars of Clay, Harry Conick Jr., Michael Buble, John Mayer…."

He pulled a Casting Crowns CD from his case, laughing at her response. "Good girl. Now that wasn't hard, was it?"

His hand was on the clutch when she gently placed hers over it to get his attention. The touch sent tingles up and down his arm. He looked at her. Her voice was barely above a whisper. "I'm not a child, David."

He took his hand off the gear shift and placed it on the steering wheel . She had no idea how aware of her womanly qualities he was; but he knew himself well enough to keep his hands otherwise occupied. "I know Lexy. But I want you to be honest with me. I can take what you have to say. I promise."

She nodded and he quickly put the car in reverse. If he didn't get her somewhere public quick he wasn't going to be able to control himself.

Dinner was at a quaint restaurant in Augusta that had a fabulous reputation. Its specialty was apparently surf and turf, and she had to agree after finishing off a decadent piece of filet mignon, whatever accolades the restaurant received were more than deserved. The lighting was low and soft jazz played over the sound system. People sat around, mostly couples, talking softly. Conversation was flowing easily; Lexy was grateful, she thought after the first tender moments in the car all they would do is stare at one another or challenge each other. Neither was good in her eyes. But thankfully, the two had discussed the camp and David's job, but had not really delved into anything too serious. David ordered two lattes and his recommendation for dessert. Several of the employees seemed to know him and she found herself wondering how many times he patronized the rather expensive dining. As if he read her mind, he commented. "I know the owner of the place rather well. Actually, he is the uncle of one of my former players."

Lexy raised her eyebrows. "Ahhh, I see." She took a sip of her water.

David leaned back, his sport coat hanging on the chair beside her. "So, tell me about your family. I know you have two brothers. What else?"

A twinge of homesickness overcame her at the mention of the people she loved more than anything else. It was hard to believe she hadn't seen them in over a month. "My mom and dad met in college and have been married ever since. They are completely in love, can't keep their hands off one another sometimes, much to my horror as a teenager."

David laughed, his eyes dancing as he listened.

"My dad is a judge, and my mom is a homemaker who dabbles in legal consulting. I have two older brothers who as you can guess protected me fiercely growing up."

David could only imagine.

"They are actually about your age, so six years difference definitely categorized me as a baby sister."

"Your brothers are twins?"

Lexy looked surprised. "Yeah. I thought I told you that, sorry."

"Anyway, Brad is a football coach and lives close to my mom and dad. He is married, but with no kids. I think they are going to start trying next year. Billy is a missionary out in Africa."

David's eyes got big as he leaned forward. "Your brothers' names are Brad and Billy King?"

"Yeees….that's what I said. What's wrong?"

"Where did they go to school?"

Lexy giggled. "Much to my parents' delight they played football at The University of Georgia. They both got partial scholarships." Without thinking, she put her hand over his. "What's wrong?"

He didn't take his eyes off their hands for several seconds. Then, much to her dismay, he removed his hand and rested it on the table. "Lexy, I know your brothers. They were friends of mine in college. I played at UGA too."

Lexy slapped the table and made her silverware jump. She looked around, embarrassed at the thump it made and covered her mouth with her hand. "Sorry." She looked at David and replied in a whisper. "You are kidding me? You know them?" She shook her head. "That is unbelievable! What a small world…" The server brought two pieces of the most divine chocolate cake she had ever seen along with two lattes topped with whip cream. They began eating, but Lexy noticed a definite change in David. She wondered what was wrong. For the remainder of the dinner they made small talk, friendly but different than what had been flirtatious exchanges before. Lexy was picking at her cake when David suggested they go. She nodded and as he guided her out of the restaurant.

Chapter 8

Lexy King. He should have made the
connection with Billy and Brad. It wasn't
that he didn't like the twins; in fact, their
influence helped changed his life. At first,
they weren't really part of his crowd, he
usually hung out with the typical fraternity
type, but watching Brad and Billy interact
with the other team members, while still
maintaining their witness spoke to David.
David wasn't a bad guy, but was the
stereotypical college student. He liked girls
and he liked to party. He never went over the
edge, but he also wasn't afraid to get close.
One afternoon, after practice, the brothers
had asked him to come to their apartment and
hang out. They did and soon a friendship
formed. Over some intense basketball
games, they got to know one another.
Neither of them was judgmental about the
way David lived his life, but they did ask him
about his choices. Both guys walked the line
of being a true friend without passing
judgment. It was rare. But David wasn't
ready to change his life. Then one day his
mom and called to tell him about Tommy's
diagnosis. David went straight to the library
and researched Cystic Fibrosis. After three
hours of reading about terrifying symptoms

and mortality rates, he couldn't see for the blinding tears of anger. It didn't seem fair; Tommy was an innocent nine year old. David walked over to the guys' apartment, desperate to talk to someone. Billy was the only one home. After several long hours, Billy shared God's grace and mercy with David. David had heard the plan of salvation before. His family didn't go to church regularly, but on occasion he would attend Vacation Bible School to give his mom a break. At this point in his life, salvation seemed like someone tossing him a lifejacket to rescue him from flailing about in doubt and anger. That night David prayed to accept Christ. Brad and Billy helped him grow as a believer the remainder of the year, but after college, they lost touch. Both guys had gone back to Jacksonville, and he had met Macy and decided to stay on during the summer before returning to Carolina.

Now, how ironic was that six years later, he had fallen in love with their baby sister? He couldn't help but wonder how they would feel, knowing that their former partying friend was interested in their most beloved Alexandra. He didn't feel worthy. He knew Lexy's upbringing. The girl had probably never walked off the narrow path in her life. She deserved someone who was like her.

Probably someone like Brody, the guy she supposedly broke up with.

He pulled into the parking lot near the river walk and turned off the car. He looked over at Lexy who was staring at his profile. She looked hurt and confused. "What is it, David?"

He shook his head. "Nothing, Lexy. Come on."

He walked around the car and opened her door for her. She got out. He didn't reach for her hand, but instead put his in his pockets. Together, they walked slowly along the river. The soft whisper of a gentle breeze tickled their ears. It was warm, but not unpleasant. Lexy stopped at a lookout spot and leaned against the railing. With a quiet sigh she turned and rested her elbows on the iron barrier. She looked in the sky and David couldn't help but notice the way her long hair hung, reaching towards the rippling Savannah River. She turned to him and said one word. "Truth."

He knew she was right. He leaned on one elbow and faced her. "Your brother, Billy, led me to Christ in college

Lexy bit her bottom lip and smiled. "Really?"

"Yep. Really." He turned back towards the water staring into the dark of night.

She turned around next to him. "So…."

He shook his head. "You're perfect, Lexy. Your brothers were perfect. Your parents are probably perfect." He looked at her wide eyed expression. "I wasn't."

"What are you talking about, David?"

"My life up to my senior year wasn't any where near perfect. I was reckless and irresponsible. I had a lot of anger. My dad left when I was in high school, my mom was struggling with Tommy who was sick all the time." He shook his head and she could hear the emotion in his voice. "I made a lot of bad choices."

She touched his arm. "So do we all, David. None of my family is perfect."

"When did you accept Christ, Lexy?"

She closed her eyes as if she knew what he was thinking. "When I was seven."

He huffed. "See? You were a child, and I'm sure you never strayed much." He walked to the other side of the walk and turned towards her. "You deserve someone better."

At first, he took her silence as agreement, but even in the dark he could see her slow boil to anger, and when her hands landed on her hips he knew he had stepped over a line. "Don't you dare put me on some kind of pedestal. Don't you dare make my salvation any less miraculous than yours. I am not perfect, have never been. And I've got news for you; neither of us will ever be perfect. I am flesh and blood just like you and Christ died for me just like you." Her voice was getting a little louder. A couple of people were looking their way. He decided it would be smart to close some of the distance between them. She in turn lowered her voice to a harsh whisper. "And Christ changed you like he changed me. As far as what or whom I deserve, you need to leave that between me and God. You're right. I have been His for a very long time, and I have full confidence He has chosen someone for me." She pointed to him, then back to herself. "You and I don't have anything right now besides a very dear friendship, one that I have come to cherish very much. And don't ever sell God short in the work He has done in you. True, I didn't know you in college. But I know you now. I see you start every day praying on the bleachers and reading your Bible. I see you with the kids, and with Jo and Frannie. I know how your character has been tested, and how God saw you through it. You have been nothing but honorable in your actions towards me, even if you are a little, ok a lot arrogant sometimes. And tonight, whatever

this is, will go wherever God wants it to go."
She finally stopped for breath.

David was sure she would eventually pass
out if she didn't stop. He placed each hand
on either side of her face. "Are you
finished?"

She took a deep breath and whispered.
"Yes."

They were so close, he could feel her
breath on his face. He wanted to kiss her so
badly. David bent his knees to see her better
when she looked down at the boardwalk. *Oh,
please Lord. I don't want to scare her.* He
tilted her chin up to him and searched her
eyes. "Lexy?"

She ducked underneath his arm and moved
inside the gazebo. He followed her and
gently touched her arm until she turned
around. Then he saw a trembling chin and
the glistening of tears on her face. And then
it hit him. She was scared, not of him, but of
the kiss. It was hard to believe a beautiful
twenty two year old woman in 2008 had
never been kissed, but he supposed it was
possible. Was that it? His voice was soft as
he took her into his arms. She rolled her
eyes and laughed at herself as she wiped the
tears from her face. "I'm so stupid. I can't
believe I'm crying."

He kept his arms around her but pulled away so he could see her face. "You never kissed your boyfriend?"

She, blushed, sighed, and looked out over the river. "Yes, David. I kissed my boyfriend."

He kept his voice soft. "Then what is it?"

When she finally met his gaze, he saw pure honesty. "Brody isn't *you*, David. Brody and I were close, and we did share a few kisses, but they were more friendly than not." She gulped and tried to focus on David's eyes. "I never really wanted Brody to kiss me. I never wanted to kiss him back. I didn't know it then, but I know it now. I never loved him, never felt what I should have felt…" She paused and he waited. "For the first time ever, my heart is beating fast and my palms are sweaty. I can't think straight. I…."

He couldn't stand it any more. He cut her off with the most gentle and unchaste kiss he could master. After a few seconds he could feel her hands come up around his neck and a groan escape from his throat. Suddenly he knew he was in dangerous waters with Alexandra King. The desires she stirred in him were powerful, but she wasn't his to love and it took every bit of will power he had to remember that, as he pulled back and put some distance between them. He gently released himself from her embrace and walked back towards the guardrail.

She was breathing hard, reluctant to let him go, but teased. "You have a bad habit of cutting me off."

He sat down on the nearest bench, wanting to hold her again, but also knowing he had limits. He couldn't help but smile. "Are you complaining?"

"No." She cocked her head and underneath the moonlight with her ringlets and sparkling eyes, she looked like an angel.

He got up, walked towards her and reached for her hand. "Come on young lady. Let me get you home before the dynamic duo of Jo and Fran take out a warrant for my arrest."

Her face showed disappointment but she didn't argue as they walked to the car without saying a word.

They were riding down the Riverwatch Expressway holding hands and listening to the smooth sound of the Mustang's engine. Lexy didn't know what any of this meant, and she wasn't sure she wanted to talk about it. These moments, in his car, holding his hand were too precious. She was scared about the next couple of weeks, but she felt safe, too. Kissing David was like being surprised with a gift she had always dreamed of, wrapped in the most beautiful package. Everything about him seemed right. Almost everything.

She looked over at him, and for the first time since she had met him, his expression seemed peaceful. "When is Tommy arriving?"

He smiled, one of a doting older brother. "He gets here tomorrow. My mom is driving him down, spending the night, then heading back to Carolina Sunday night. I can't wait for you to meet Tommy on Monday. He's a great kid."

Lexy tried not to feel slighted that he hadn't invited her to meet his mom, but if she was honest with herself that was exactly how she felt. "Have you got big plans?"

"Yeah. We're going to do church on Sunday night…"

"What is the name of your church again?" Jo and Frannie had mentioned it before, but she couldn't remember. All she knew was that it wasn't Grace Baptist where she had been attending with them.

"Warren Baptist Church. It's in Augusta, probably about twenty minutes from Jo and Fran. It's a big church with a lot of activities. I think Tommy will make some friends in the youth group while he is here."

Again, no invitation to church. *Stop it, Lexy.* "Ok, go ahead. I cut you off; I'm sorry."

He caressed her thumb with his finger. "That's ok. Well, there is camp, of course, and he's going to help me with football preparations…"

She decided to change the subject. "Are you excited about the season?"

David's expression changed from one of joy to troubled as they pulled up into Jo and Fran's driveway. He turned the car off and faced her; even in the dim light of the dashboard she could tell the mention of football set him on edge. That troubled her. Wasn't he supposed to love the sport? "What is it, David?"

He shook his head and then stopped. "I can't lie to you, Lexy. I won't play games." He reached out and touched her freckled cheek and then quickly removed his hand as if an electrical current had shocked him. "I haven't been able to focus on the season like I should. The negatives have kind of taken over; because nothing about the job is as exciting as the time I spend with you. And you are leaving in two weeks."

Lexy's heartbeat began to play a cadence and her hands suddenly felt like she had dipped them in a river of fear. What was he talking about? They had been out on one date. How could she make a difference in the way he felt about something he had been doing his whole career? But the truth was that his feelings mirrored her own. She missed her family, but she would ache for David, and that reality scared her more than anything else. *God, what is happening?* She turned to face him, trying to find the right words, but he was right; she couldn't play games with him either. Lexy knew she would go home at the end of the two weeks. Jacksonville was where she belonged. There were too many unknowns in Augusta. "I know." It was barely a whisper, but he heard her.

He nodded as if something had been settled. Apparently, David was done talking. He walked over to her side of the car, opened the door and walked her up the steps. She invited him in, but he declined. It was getting late, but there was something else. The light in David's eyes had gone off and the warmth that filled her on the river walk had faded to a chill. He hugged her and kissed the top of her head. She turned and

closed the door on what could have been a
perfect night.

David drove entirely too fast on the way
home. Why did he allow himself to fall in
love with her? He knew from the beginning
she was only here for eight weeks. She had
never mentioned the possibility of staying,
and he wouldn't dream of asking her to give
up the loving family and friends in a city she
loved; for what, to be a coach's wife? He
laughed aloud. Was he delusional enough to
believe that Alexandra Lynne King, daughter
of a prominent judge, would actually
consider vowing till death do us part and take
a vow of poverty? He ran his fingers through
his hair. "David, you really have gone over
the edge, man." No, the best thing he could
do is put her out of his mind. And as he
closed his eyes that night he knew the harsh
truth. Putting her out of his mind was one
thing, but his heart had a mind of its own.

Lexy woke up from a fitful night of sleeping.
She had prayed and drifted off around one in
the morning. Her head hurt, her eyes hurt,
and most of all her heart hurt. If falling in
love with a man she could never have was

spreading her wings, she would have been satisfied with a clipping six weeks ago. Lexy stretched and walked to the window that overlooked the driveway. It was just last night that the beautiful red car holding the beautiful man dropped her off; it was just last night that he kissed her. Her first real kiss. And it was just last night that reality doused both of them with the cold truth. He was headed one way, and she clearly another. Lexy wasn't even sure where, if anywhere, her career would go. Talk of being an educator did not leave her with a peaceful feeling; instead it left her feeling hopeless, like she was entering a field where she would work her fingers to the bone and not make a difference. Lexy sighed; she knew she needed some time with God. It was the only way to gain much needed perspective. She kept on her oversized pajamas, grabbed her journal and Bible and walked down the steps fully expecting to find Fran and Jo waiting for a full report. But when she opened the door the house was wrapped in the silence of morning. Lexy glanced at the clock on the stove and gasped. It was 8:30! She never slept that late. Then, she saw a note written in Jo's handwriting.

Lexy,

We decided to go to Atlanta for the day to visit family. We were going to ask you to join us but didn't have the heart to wake you. We'll be back before dinner and can't wait to hear about last night.

Love,

Jo and Frannie

Lexy took a deep breath and walked onto the covered porch, and took a seat on the swing. Peaches was glad to see her, apparently thankful to be outside for a little while. Maybe being alone for the morning was just as well. It would give her time to think and pray, to ask God for peace. Lexy opened her Bible and turned to a verse in Isaiah, one that she always read when she was tired and confused. *Even youths grow tired and weary, and young men stumble and fall; but those who hope in the Lord will renew their strength. They will soar on wings like eagles; they will run and not grow weary, they will walk and not be faint.* Lexy inhaled the wisdom in the scripture and prayed for God's guidance. She then turned to the passage she had been studying in Proverbs. There was one particular verse she had been thinking about. She moved her index finger down the page until she located the right one. *Aha.* Verse 25. *She is clothed with strength and dignity; she can laugh at the days to come.* Lexy closed her Bible and opened her journal. She began to write, anxiously unloading her thoughts on the paper.

Strength and dignity….laughter. To me, they seem totally unrelated. Lord, when I think of strength I think of endurance and stamina. Dignity conjures up images of someone with their head held high, someone who is above worldliness and answers to God alone.

Then laughter; not nervous laughter or giggling, but laughter that comes from joy….I want to understand, God. I want to know how to clothe myself with Godly strength and dignity while laughing at the days to come, knowing you will fight any battles for me. I know trust and obedience are a major part of the equation. Help me to obey when it comes to David. I want to go to him and give him my heart. I want to rest in his embrace, but what I should want more is to rest in yours. It isn't that I think he's wrong for me, but I have a feeling there is something I'm supposed to do first. You go before us all, Jesus. I know all these things with my head, Lord. Help me know them in my heart.

David drove to Jo and Frannie's with a heavy heart. He had not slept well; he felt like his heart had been stolen by a thief in the night, but the truth was he had given it away. And as he pulled up into their driveway for the third time in twenty four hours, he couldn't believe he was returning to the scene of the crime. But he had made a promise to Jo and Frannie that he would take care of their yard for them. And since Lexy had come to stay, he had neglected his duties. No, he would do the job, and then leave. Maybe she was asleep, or maybe she went to Atlanta with Jo and Fran. He knew they were making a trip today. He walked around to the side door of the garage and used the key he kept on his ring. He retrieved the equipment and finished up the front yard and flower beds in no time. He drove around to the back only to be stopped cold by the sight of Lexy staring at him from the back porch. She smiled as Peaches commenced to attacking his leg. David tried to gently kick the "wanna be" dog off of him, but Peaches was obviously smitten and wouldn't let go. He could hear Lexy laughing from the swing, and despite his mood, he laughed too. Finally, the puffball released him and took care of some delicate business in one of the nearby bushes. He had reached the back steps leading to the porch and looked up to find Lexy with an open Bible and journal sitting beside her.

"Hi." Her voice was scratchy, almost like she had been crying. The thought smashed the pieces of his already broken heart.

"Hi." She looked adorable in her oversized pajamas and messy hair. He wanted to go sit beside her on the swing and take her into his arms, but he didn't.

"I, uh, come and mow the lawn for Jo and Fran every other week."

She glanced at the mower and at him; suddenly, he was aware he didn't have a shirt on and probably looked like he had been rolling in the dirt. He took the shirt hanging over his shoulder and quickly slipped it over his head. She watched him before whispering. "I figured."

He sat down in the Adirondack chair across from the swing. He looked down at his hands and then back at her. "Lexy, I, well, I'm sorry about last night."

She looked down at her Bible and journal. "Yeah. Me too."

He closed his eyes briefly and when he looked at her he saw his frustrations mirrored in hers. "I care for you very much, Lexy."

"I know, David. I feel the same way."

"But?"

"But?"

He swallowed, not wanting to voice what the truth was. "The timing is wrong."

She nodded her head. Several seconds passed before she commented. "Timing is never wrong for a friendship, David. The rest isn't up to us."

He smiled, one that didn't reach his eyes, but it was the best he could do. "So, for the next two weeks...."

She smiled mischievously. "I'll be your friend, if you'll be mine."

"Sounds good."

She changed the subject. "When does Tommy get here?"

"Some time after lunch."

"I look forward to getting to know him."

David nodded. "I would like that."

"But maybe we should put off our morning meetings so you can spend some time with him alone."

David laughed lightly and got up. "Tommy doesn't get up before 8:30..." He looked at Lexy with some sadness. "..besides those morning meetings make my day."

She got up from the swing and his heart skipped a couple of beats. "Mine too, David."

"So…see you on Monday?"

She opened the back door and stepped inside. "Monday, it is."

Lexy smiled as Jo and Frannie chatted nonstop about their day visiting family in Atlanta. She listened to entertaining antics about elderly aunts and zany cousins, but the funniest story was about Jo's crazy sister, Marta. Marta did not suffer from Alzheimer's or Schizophrenia. Apparently, no personality disorder had been invented to fit her personality. She was just nutty, as described by her very educated sibling. Marta liked cats and had a dozen of them milling around her old Georgia mansion. After her wealthy entrepreneur of a husband passed away, Marta kept a full house of servants ready to answer her strange requests at every beck and call. When Fran and Jo arrived, Ms. Hattie, who had been the maid for forty years answered the door with a look of warning. And when the two cousins rounded the corner, they knew why. Despite the temperature in the triple digits, Marta was dressed in a fur coat, jewels, and high heels.

She was watching, apparently very amused, while the butler and chauffer narrated a play acted out by none other than her cats, who had been dressed for their assigned roles. Well, needless to say Jo and Fran took their tea immediately and sat down, whereby Marta insisted they stay for the remainder of the show. They did but scurried out of there in a record time of fifteen minutes, thankfully checking the family visit off their list.

Lexy started crying from laughing so hard, but then to her dismay, once the tears started flowing there was no stopping them. Jo and Frannie stopped their story telling long enough to look at one another for confirmation that their Lexy was having a meltdown. Fran jumped up from the couch and grabbed some tissue. Lexy gratefully accepted it and tried to calm herself down as Jo moved next to her in an attempt to hug her.

Sniffles escaped Lexy's mouth while she kneaded the tissue paper. "I don't know what's wrong with me."

Fran patted her hand. "Why don't you start out by telling us about last night. How did it go?"

Lexy sighed and threw her head on the back of the couch. "It was wonderful and horrible all at the same time."

They listened as Lexy relayed the events of the evening and morning. She threw her tissue beside her and shrugged her shoulders. "And that's it. The timing's wrong and we're done."

Moments passed before the usual soft-spoken Frannie spoke up with an exasperated tone. "Well, that has to be the dumbest thing I have ever heard in my life!"

Jo's mouth fell open and Lexy stared. "Frannie!!"

Fran started moving around the room, pacing. Her gaze at Lexy was like one of the firing squad. "Do you like him?"

"Yes. I like him." Lexy's feelings went deeper than like, but she wasn't sure how to say it.

Jo chimed in. "And we know he likes you…."

Lexy nodded her head in confusion. What was this, good cop, bad cop?

Fran stomped her foot and looked at her cousin. "Of course he does, he said he l…"

Jo cut Frannie off. "I think the two of you are being smart."

Lexy and Frannie turned their heads towards Jo. "You do?"

Jo gave Frannie a look of warning. "Yes. You're young. Take it slow. If it's meant to be, it will be." She hopped up off the couch and bent to kiss Lexy. "I think I'll go to bed now. Goodnight dear." She turned to Frannie who was still open mouthed. "You should go to bed too, Fran."

"But…"

Fran stopped her rebuttal, shook her head and bid Lexy goodnight. Lexy walked up to her loft determined to pray for peace but she was asleep before her head hit the pillow.

Chapter 9

The gym bag landed with a thump in the red jeep as Lexy took a deep, cleansing breath. She stretched, thanking God for the endorphins that danced through her veins. It had been a good morning; she and David opted to jog for an hour before camp. The easy pace they had long since established was complemented by the comfortable silence. Talking had become an option, not a requirement and Lexy liked it that way. And now, as she turned around and headed towards the school, she couldn't help but hum an anonymous tune from her childhood. However, her humming came to a halt when she saw David walking toward her with what looked like a younger version of himself--- Tommy. Except Tommy wasn't what she expected; she had envisioned someone sick and coughing, maybe pale and thin. Granted, he was thin and the few times he coughed during his approach towards her she resisted the urge to cringe, but his smile and his eyes overshadowed any signs of illness. He was fully alive and joyful and apparently very excited about meeting her. His hand was out ready to greet her five feet away. David glowed with pride as he introduced her to his baby brother.

Tommy laughed as the same emerald green eyes danced with an irresistible urge to tease. "I have heard so much about you. It is so nice to finally meet the girl who knocked my brother upside the head."

David put him in a head lock while Lexy tried to control her blushing. "That's me."

David released him reluctantly so Lexy could give him a sisterly hug. "It's good to meet you too, Tommy. Thank you for wanting to help out with the camp. The kids will be thrilled to get to know you; they love your brother." As do I…

The unspoken words hung in the air. Somehow David understood and began to shuffle his feet. He turned to Tommy. "Come on, kid. Let's get set up for the day. We don't want to get in trouble with the director. She runs a tight ship."

Lexy laughed and shook her head. Tommy followed, but turned back and gave her a playful wink.

David couldn't help but be proud of Tommy. Initially, he was horrified at Tommy's pale complexion and painful cough, but after a couple of hours David stood back in awe at his kid brother's attitude toward life. Tommy was completely aware of the daunting diagnosis and lived the effects daily, but he was determined to make the most of everyday and live for the One who made him. If only his mother had that kind of faith. David and his mother talked Sunday afternoon as Tommy played some video games. They walked out to David's truck when Rita, their mother, looked at him with a worried expression.

Her tall stature hung with the weight of her son's illness. "He's getting worse, David."

David hugged her in an attempt to comfort. "I know."

She shook her head sadly. "We're doing everything we can for him."

"I know, Mom."

She pulled away from him and pushed herself up onto the tailgate. She was silent for several seconds. When she looked up at him, her tired brown eyes were swimming in a pain David could only pray he would never know, the pain of watching a child slip from the fingertips of life. Her voice was barely more than a hoarse whisper. "It's not enough."

David pushed past the emotion that was building in his throat as he sat beside his mother. There was so much he wanted to say to her; despite his and Tommy's faith, Rita was not a believer. She was selfless and compassionate, but had no faith. David prayed for the destruction of the wall composed of betrayal and sorrow that had taken root in his mother's heart; but year after year she remained blind to the truth. And now, when she needed Jesus, all he could offer was his inadequate shoulder. "Tommy seems at peace, Mom."

David couldn't help but note the flash of anger as his mother raked through her dark brown hair. "Oh, he is. He tells me that all the time. It's almost like he's ready whenever the time comes." The laugh that escaped her was not one of humor but angry frustration. "It's like he wants to go, and all he does is read the Bible and talk of heaven. He spends more time trying to get me to see the light than concentrating on fighting his own illness." Rita hopped down from the truck and looked at David with an intensity he had never seen before. Chills ran races up and down his arms. "I'll never forgive God if he dies. I'll go to hell just to spite Him." And as David watched his mother walk away, he closed his eyes and prayed like he never prayed before. Then he realized her statement gave him hope. She did have a relationship with God; it was one built on anger, but it was a dialogue, nonetheless.

Early the next morning David got his mother loaded up, received instructions regarding Tommy's breathing treatments, and said a prayer as he watched her drive away. He looked over at his brother and smiled. Tommy returned his look with a sideways hug. "I know. I'm praying for her. Maybe God will use this time away from worrying about me to work on her heart."

David turned and walked with his brother toward the house. "She'll never stop worrying about you. She'll never stop worrying about me either. That's how moms work, I guess. But you're right; this time alone may be just what God had in mind."

The fireworks exploded with pops of reds, greens, golds, and blues. This Fourth of July had been delightful. At first, when Tommy invited her to a cook out at David's cabin on the lake, Lexy was skeptical. Why was she going to put herself through this kind of torture? The more time she spent with him, the more tears she would shed on the way home. She was sure of it. But when Jo and Frannie said it was a tradition and that they were going too, well, what choice did she have? But now, as Lexy sat on the beach and watched the display of color in the sky coupled with the peacefulness of the lake, she was so grateful she had come. The five of them finished cleaning up after the delicious barbeque, and Jo and Frannie took off. They asked David to bring Lexy home later, because after all, they were sure it was too early for her to turn in. Lexy had been embarrassed and made a face at the ladies to let them know her displeasure, but they just smiled and toddled away, seemingly pleased with themselves. And now here she was, enjoying the concert of critters around her. As a kid, she always loved to camp and David's little shack of a cabin reminded her of some of the places they used to go as a family. She was truly at home. Lexy looked down the beach and noticed the soft glow of a fire. David had given Tommy an assignment of building a fire, and apparently David had gone to oversee the project. She wiped off the back of her shorts and walked down the beach a few feet to join the two brothers.

Tommy looked at David hopefully when a few of the teenagers down the beach armed with guitars had asked if Tommy could join them.

David nodded and they both watched as he ran off to join his buddies. David looked over at Lexy. "They're from the youth group at church."

Lexy nodded. "Yeah. I figured." She watched Tommy a bit longer. "He's a good kid David."

He was watching her and smiled at the observation. "Yeah. I think so, too."

David's slow movement towards her and taking her hand in his didn't feel strange. Neither did sitting beside him basking in the glow of the fire, being silent as the bursts of celebration hung in the air. Being with him felt natural. It felt right. David released her hand and leaned back on his arms, stretching his legs out in front of him. He was looking at the back of her head when he spoke.

"Do you miss home, Lexy?"

She let a handful of sand sift through her fingers and tried not to move when David casually fingered a curly lock of her hair, playing with it. "Yes."

"What will you do?"

All she could do was shrug her shoulders.

"That's not much of a plan."

Her gaze shifted to the sky. "Ha. I agree. God and I have been talking a lot. He's got me on hold right now."

David had let go of her hair but she could still feel his gaze on her back. Finally, he sat up and gently turned her face towards him.

"I'm glad you're praying about it." His voice was so soft, almost a whisper. "I want you to know I'm praying for you too. As much as I want you to stay, I want what He wants for you even more. I want you to have joy and peace, whatever that means."

David's eyes held so much promise and adoration that Lexy didn't know whether to start crying or leap up and run to try to salvage what was left of her heart. But before she could make a decision, he moved forward and the expectation of his kiss sent her reeling. And this time there were no tears; this time she was ready. But what she wasn't expecting was the rush of blood that went straight to her head as his gentle kiss turned more intense. She could feel everything in her respond and for the first time in her life she understood what getting lost in the moment meant. She had risen to her knees and had her hands in his hair; her eyes were watering, a sensation of dizziness swept over her; and at that moment, David stood up, very nearly making her fall to the sand. He walked to the water, with his back to her, and as she moved closer she could see his shoulders shaking.

"David?" She reached out to touch him and when he turned to her he looked angry.

"I'm so sorry, Lexy. I shouldn't have kissed you." It was obvious he was mad at himself. Lexy wanted to make him feel better, to somehow lighten the moment.

She bit her bottom lip and said in a stage whisper. "I think I kissed you back, David."

She saw his shoulders relax as he moved towards her and placed his hand on the side of her cheek, slightly smiling. "Yeah, you did. But regardless of my actions, I did mean what I said. At least I know I should mean it. I do want what God wants for you, Lexy. I really do." He placed her hand over his heart; she could feel the rapid beating and was sure it echoed her own. "I've prayed for you, for me, for us."

She shook her head and looked down at the water. "Oh, David. So have I."

He pulled her to him but held back so he could see her face. "And I think you and I have both received the same answer, right?"

She nodded, this time letting the tears flow freely.

"So, sometimes obedience means sacrifice."

Again she nodded.

David reached down and kissed the top of her head. "Let me take you home, Lexy."

It took everything in her to pull away from his embrace, but in the end she knew they couldn't be here alone another second without looking back with life long regret. "Ok, David. Ok."

It was her last Saturday in Augusta, and Lexy had enjoyed the morning of shopping and now lunch with Laura and Karen. Karen, a chatty mother of two, and a teaching veteran was busily checking off back to school items off her list, when Laura looked at Lexy and asked a million dollar question.

"So what next, Lexy?"

Lexy took a big gulp of her sweet tea before answering the question that had defined her thoughts. "I don't really know. I'm going to go back to Jacksonville. That is a definite."

Karen and Laura looked at one another and responded in unison. "Why?"

Lexy picked at her salad. "I have to go figure some things out."

"Don't you want to stay?" This came from Karen, who had now put the list aside.

"Sure. I would love to stay, but I just can't just pick up and move with unanswered questions and a bunch of insecurities. I have to think on in it, pray on it; it wouldn't be fair otherwise."

Laura ventured. "Fair to whom?"

Lexy smiled, shrugging her shoulders. She knew what her friend was implying. They had already asked questions about her and David. She had been honest; they were friends, friends with plenty of potential to become something more. "Yes. David, me, my career, my family and friends back home….the timing is wrong right now."

"Will you teach in Jacksonville?"

"That's just it. I haven't decided yet."

Laura shook her head as she signed the bill for lunch. "Education is a tough field, Lexy. I won't lie to you. But there are a lot of advantages to the profession, not to mention a lot of opportunities. You should think about it."

And as Lexy lay her head down later that night, Laura's words replayed in her mind.

David tossed and turned not being able to shake the feeling time was escaping him. But what was he supposed to do? True, he loved Lexy. He knew it. He had only known her six weeks, but they had spent so much time together, it felt like months. The idea of waking up and not anticipating seeing her, hearing her bubbly voice, watching her face transform when faced with a little competition, well to say it depressed him was a gross understatement. Even his little brother was keenly aware of his situation. He couldn't help but smile when he thought back on the day after the Fourth of July cook out. When they entered David's house after driving back from the cabin, Tommy went straight to the kitchen and fixed himself a snack. David laughed at the growing mountain of food on his kid brother's plate. It was true that people with CF were supposed to eat more than the regular caloric intake, but he thought Tommy might be taking it to the next level. He moved next to him and poured him a glass of milk, grabbing an apple and a bag of chips for himself. They sat across the table from one another concentrating on their food for a few moments. Finally, Tommy looked up with a mouthful of club sandwich. "So, what's up with you and Lexy?"

David almost choked on his chip. "Excuse me?"

"Oh, yeah right. You really expect me to believe the just friends speech. Give me a little more credit than that."

David rolled his eyes. "Oh, I give you plenty of credit. That's why you're getting nothing out of me. She's a great girl, albeit with some irritating flaws. I like her and respect her. End of story."

Tommy chewed and swallowed. "Then you're stupid." He took another big bite and a swig of milk as if he hadn't just insulted his older and much bigger brother.

"How am I stupid, Tommy?"

The tone in David's voice was harsh; Tommy had hit a sensitive spot, one he didn't want to think about. "She's only here for a couple of weeks. I have school, my job. She has a life. In my mind I'm being pretty smart."

Tommy wiped his mouth and sat back in his chair. "Are you telling me you don't think God put Lexy in your life on purpose? You have been ticked ever since the Becky thing, walking around with a chip on your shoulder…"

David put his hand up in protest. "Now wait…"

"No, you wait, big brother. I love you and respect you very much. But you've got a good thing in front of you with Lexy. Do you see how you look at her, how she looks at you? She is perfect for you. What's tying you to Augusta anyway? You moved away from your own hometown for Macy, and if you ask me…"

"I didn't ask you."

Tommy got up to rinse his plate. "No, you didn't. But bringing your attention to things you are too blind to see is my job. Lexy is for keeps, man."

As David pushed back from the table, he realized his brother had a point. But it was too complicated to be solved over a snack in his kitchen. "You're a kid, Tommy. There's a lot more to it."

The look on Tommy's face wasn't one of a fifteen year old; it was one of an older, much wiser man. "Maybe you're right, David. But don't you think she's worth trying to figure it out?"

And those words had played in his head over and over again. Of course she was worth it. But Lexy could stay if she wanted to. He remembered Jo saying something about ten special education positions available for the fall. Lexy had to know that. If she really wanted to be with him wouldn't she apply for a job? The nagging reminder of his unconfessed love for her tugged on his heart, but she knew, right? After the other night, she had to know. Besides, David knew leaving was breaking her heart. That was evident. She felt something for him, but was he the man for her? Was God sending her on a straight path back to who He has chosen? David turned over, and put his fist in the pillow, and attempted to pray the hardest prayer he had ever uttered. One that would put him out of the picture if he wasn't God's man for her.

The final week of camp was here and Lexy could hardly believe her time in Augusta was almost over. Back to school sales signaled summer was coming to an end and with it the eight weeks of independence she had enjoyed. Summer football practice would begin on Thursday afternoon; her and David's time in the morning would officially come to an end. She already missed him; her heart ached for the anticipated absence of his soft smiles and gentle hugs. Lexy even knew she would miss the teasing she received from her gentle giant. Her gentle giant. She knew that wasn't quite accurate, but she knew David would always hold a place in her heart. But Saturday would bring the ride back to Jacksonville, and she knew she had to go. Part of her had daydreamed about applying for a teaching position, living with Jo and Frannie, and staying to pursue whatever might be between her and David. But she prayed about it and staying didn't seem right. She had no idea what God was going to do with her career. She missed her parents, friends, and even Brody. The bottom line was she had unfinished business in Jacksonville; she needed to go back and reassess her life.

Lexy shook her head as she walked toward the gym. She had a real talent for worrying about what tomorrow would bring before today's delivery of events had arrived. She had one more week as Camp Courage's director and she was determined to make it a good one. The camp would go about their normal activities until Friday, and then on Friday she would have the final cook out. All of the parents, along with volunteers and campers would be attending. Lexy glanced at her watch and realized she had to go pick up the drinks and paper products that had been donated for Friday's events. Maybe David would let her borrow his truck. Lexy entered the gym and smiled at the scene that met her. David and Tommy were playing kick ball with the preschool Pups. Her heart melted when David scooped up Bennie; one of the four year olds with Down syndrome and ran with him as he was giggling uncontrollably toward home base. Bennie beamed at David as Tommy rushed over to give them both a high five. Her own laughter bubbled up, catching David's attention. He gently placed Bennie back down, and headed over to her wearing a devastating smile that succeeded in waking up all her pet butterflies.

"Hi." She wanted to save the mental picture of him. He was dressed in his coaching clothes, wearing his hat and whistle, but his facial expression was one of contentment and joy. He had never looked as handsome as he did in that moment.

"Hi, yourself." He wiped the sweat from his brow on his shirt sleeve. "How's it going?"

"Good." They were toe to toe now and Lexy looked fully into his face. She had the overwhelming desire to stand on her tip toes, throw her arms around his neck and lay one on him; but she didn't. "Do you think I could borrow your truck to go pick up some supplies for Friday?"

He hesitated and looked around, glancing at his watch. "Um, yeah. That would be fine, I guess."

Lexy's brow furrowed. "You guess? Were you going somewhere? If so, I can figure something else out."

He shook his head. "No. No. I wasn't going anywhere. In fact, I have a meeting with some of my players or I would go with you myself. But take Tommy. He can help load the supplies."

Lexy shook her head. "No, that's ok. I can handle loading it myself…"

David's expression stopped her. She knew him well enough to know Tommy would be going with her. "Ok, ask Tommy to meet me out there in five minutes."

He winked at her, causing her heart to skip a beat, and tossed her the keys.

Minutes later she and Tommy were driving down the road towards Wal-Mart. "Your brother doesn't trust me with his truck, does he?"

Lexy smiled in the direction of Tommy, but met her gaze with a strange expression. "No, he trusts you with his truck…."

Lexy could have sworn she heard him add, "but not his heart." She quickly glanced back over to see if Tommy was still looking at her, but he was concentrated on the view from the other window. His voice became upbeat as if the awkward moment had not occurred. "So, what are your plans when you head back to Jacksonville? Do you have a job lined up?"

Lexy bit her bottom lip before answering. She really could go the rest of her life without hearing that question again. "No, not really. I had planned on substitute teaching to feel out the field, but now I'm not sure."

Tommy's eyes were on her, but she didn't look at him. "Not sure about what?"

"The job. Teaching."

He had one eyebrow raised. "Oh." Several seconds went by. "You don't know if you want to teach?"

She shook her head. "No, I don't. There are glitches in the system that make me question whether or not it's the right place for me."

"What kind of glitches?"

How did she explain this to a fifteen year old? "Paper work, placement issues, high stakes testing. It's just that I'm not sure if I could be successful with all the red tape and beauracracy in education. That probably doesn't makes sense to you."

Tommy looked down at his knees and then looked up at her. She had pulled into a parking space by now and turned towards him fully. He looked so much like a younger version of David, it was hard not to take him seriously, regardless of his age. She sensed he had an old soul. "I don't understand all of it. But I'm in the special ed. program at school. I'm served under that Other Health Impairment category. I've been to enough meetings to understand there are a lot of good things and a lot of bad things about education in general. But one part of it I'm pretty sure about. You're great with kids, Lexy, and you would be an awesome teacher. We, and by we, I mean kids in school, kids who need special stuff….we need more teachers who want to be there and who care about us." Lexy noticed the emotion gathering behind Tommy's eyes and had to swallow past the lump in her own throat. "There are a lot of teachers out there who don't care."

All she could do was nod and whisper a "thank-you". It was weak, but his comments spoke to her heart. As they headed back towards the school, truck loaded, Lexy knew one thing. She had to talk to Jo.

Jo must have sensed something because she was sitting at the kitchen table when Lexy got home from camp. She looked relaxed, dressed in a bright pink shirt and black capris. Her head popped up from the journal she was reading when Lexy shut the door.

"Hey, kiddo."

"Hey, Jo." Lexy threw her satchel beside the curio cabinet and plopped down in a chair beside her friend.

Jo closed the article and gave her full attention, which was something Lexy greatly appreciated about the older woman. "What's on your mind?"

"Teaching."

Jo didn't miss a beat. "Still not sure about it, huh?"

Lexy shook her head. She could feel the tears gathering and this time she didn't try to stop them. Jo calmly handed her a tissue and placed her hand over Lexy's. "Have you enjoyed camp?"

Lexy nodded her head and blew her nose. "Very much. I love the kids."

"How much?"

"How much what?"

"How much do you love the kids?"

Lexy didn't know how to answer the question. Her brows furrowed. Finally, she shrugged her shoulders.

Jo clarified. "Do you love them enough to get paid next to nothing for planning, teaching, and grading hours and hours?"

It might be naïve, but she thought she did. "Yes."

"Do you love them enough to put up with meetings and forced volunteer work with very little thank you in return?"

Lexy thought. She thought of Noah, Daniel, and Bennie. They could be difficult, impossible even; but yeah, she loved being with them. Slowly, she nodded her head.

"Can you imagine yourself doing anything else?"

Lexy had asked herself that question a thousand times. And the truth was, no she couldn't. She didn't know if it would always be that way, but for now her heart was with the kids. She shook her head.

Jo smiled and sighed. "I've been doing this a long time, Lexy. I've worked with a lot of first year teachers. Some I knew would make a lifetime career out of it the first day I met them; others I knew wouldn't last the year. And then there was another group, one I believe you fall into. There are those people who are born teachers; they have it in them to work with kids, but at some point they choose not to do it, usually because their hearts get torn out fighting to make a difference. And only time can tell if that will happen to you, Lexy."

"So there's no way to know?"

Jo winked and chuckled. "Sure there is. You try it and give it at least three years. Make that commitment. And then reassess at the end of that time….Life is short, baby. But some things take time to decipher. Your career can and should be one of those things. It's worth it."

Lexy took a deep breath. What Jo said made sense. She could do it. She could be a teacher. There was no reason to wait and feel everything out. Tommy was right. Kids like him and Noah and Bennie and even Daniel needed good teachers. Jo interrupted her thoughts.

"So…..now that we have that settled, what about David?"

Lexy knew she looked like a deer in headlights, but honestly, she didn't know how to answer that question. What about David?

Jo continued. "Did I ever tell you about my ex-husband?"

Lexy's expression must have showed her surprise, because Jo started to laugh.

"I, well no, I assumed you were widowed."

"Oh, I am. He's dead now. But he was my ex-husband two times over."

Lexy shook her head. "I don't understand."

"I met Arnie right after college and we fell in love immediately. It was a one month whirlwind. We were married by the time we were both twenty-three. Our parents didn't approve; they thought it was too soon. They were right. We were immature and didn't know how to love one another. And at that time, neither of us had the faith that would and should have binded us together. So a very miserable few months passed before Arnie ended up getting a job in corporate America. He started traveling and was gone a lot. I, on the other hand, was at home not knowing what to do with myself. I ended up buying into a lot of the women's lib stuff that was going around. Soon, after a couple of shameful indiscretions, whatever innocence we had was long gone."

"So what happened?"

"We divorced, and then six months of misery passed, and we remarried."

"You're kidding."

Jo shook her head. "Nope. But this time it was much worse. We were clinging to one another for comfort only God can give. We kept trying to have a baby, but nothing was happening. We got frustrated. I ended up having a hysterectomy that left me scarred more emotionally than anything else. So, after a miserable eighteen months, we called it quits again."

Lexy shook her head in disbelief. "So….."

Jo looked off into space as if remembering another time and place. A slow smile spread across her face. "Fifteen years passed and on my fortieth birthday, we found each other again. This time God had come into both our lives and we had lived with Him for a long time. God honored our faith and allowed us five wonderful years together before He took Arnie home." Jo wiped away a single tear. "It was the best five years of my life."

Jo could feel the tears pooling in her own eyes at the idea of time wasted and love lost. "How did he die?"

"A heart attack. It was massive and quick. He was with Jesus before he knew what had happened, and for that I am very grateful."

Jo bit her bottom lip and cut her eyes over at Lexy.

"Why did you share that with me, Jo?"

"Because sometimes, Lexy, time is necessary. God allows time to do many things for us. Time heals and brings new life. The difference between my situation and yours is that first, we weren't believers. You and David have that going for you now. But also, I wasn't as mature as you; neither of us were. You're a smart girl. Be obedient and love; that's all we have in the present moment."

Chapter 10

David felt like his heart was being slowly ripped out of his chest with every passing day. It was Thursday morning. Lexy was leaving on Saturday. Today was their last morning together. The blanket of heaviness was palpable; he wanted to ask her to stay. But was that selfish? Is that what God wanted for her? And what if he stepped out there and asked, and she said no. With everything else that had happened in his life, he didn't know if a visual memory of Lexy rejecting him was something he wanted on file in his brain. He asked her to meet him some place different today; he wanted them to jog at the Locks. It was a beautiful setting with the dirt jogging path bordered by a wooded nature preserve and the rushing waters of the Savannah River. It was early and the sun was just beginning to make its appearance for the day. David got out of his truck and began to stretch. Several minutes passed as he tried to cheer himself up; he didn't want to set a sorrowful mood. He could hear the jeep coming down the road. Minutes later he could sense Lexy coming up behind him. Surprisingly, he felt her arms envelop him from behind and the closeness of her was enough to drive him to his knees and beg her to stay. He grasped her arms gently and slowly turned to face her. She had been crying. He touched her cheek. "What's wrong, Pup?"

Lexy looked up and smiled at the use of his nickname for her. He'd only called her that name one other time when they were playing basketball. Despite her initial protest, she liked it. Gently, she laid her head against his chest. He hugged her back, not wanting to let her go. "I'm sad." The words were simple and mumbled against his chest, but they may have well been translated from his own heart.

He kissed the top of her head. "Me too."

She looked up at him. Her eyes were misty and David knew he had to shift the momentum or this morning would be disastrous. He pulled away and took her hand in his. "Come on. I brought you here for a reason."

Lexy didn't say anything, only followed. When they descended the stairs leading down a hill and walked the short distance across the bridge, he could hear Lexy gasp. "Oh!" He smiled, not having to glance behind him to see her expression. He knew she would love it. The sun, a burst of yellows, reds, and orange coupled with the sounds of the

Savannah River was a feast for the senses. She whispered, "What is this place?"

She released his hand and moved toward the fence that shielded the Savannah River. He kept his voice soft, not wanting to interrupt nature's serenade. "It's called the Locks; its got some history behind it. Farmers used to transport their crops down the river to the mill in the city." He pointed to the bronze plaques that apparently lined the trail, detailing events of long ago. Lexy walked over to read one while he continued. "But I come here on the weekends to jog. It's nice to get lost in the sound of the water and birds." He pointed down a dirt path. "It's three miles one way, but there is a really pretty clearing at the half way point." He looked at her, asking the question with no words and smiling at the way she nodded enthusiastically. "All right, then. Let's go."

David and Lexy had long ago found their rhythm jogging beside one another. Even with his long strides, she kept up effortlessly. The jog took about fifteen minutes before they reached the clearing. It was a grassy beach where anyone could walk down to the river and stick their hands in the cool water. Lexy stopped, looking up at the early morning sky. David watched her as she walked silently to the edge of the water and sat down. He followed her, sitting down in the grass beside her. She looked at him and the pain he felt in his own heart was mirrored in her eyes. Her scratchy voice and wobbly chin barely got the words out. "I don't want to go."

He caressed her face and smiled sadly. "I don't want you to go."

She reached for his hand and he intertwined his fingers with hers. "I have to go for now."

He didn't look up at her, but focused on the way her hand fit in his. "I know you do."

She looked back at the water and sighed audibly. "David, I….."

He was about to spill his heart at her feet when the cell phone attached to her hip began to ring. She reached down to silence it, but then looked at him. "It's my mom. She never calls this early. Let me make sure nothing is wrong."

David nodded his head, showing his understanding.

She got up and walked five feet away to get better reception. He could hear the conversation from her end. "Hi, Mom. Is everything ok?"

Lexy looked over at David with a strange expression. "No, I'm not by myself."

Hairs stood up on David's arm; he didn't know why. Lexy's voice began to panic, and David stood up and moved closer. "Mom, I can't hear you. All I heard was Brody's name. What is going on?"

Lexy listened and David saw tears form and spill from her lashes one by one. He put his hand on her shoulder as she nodded her head. "Ok, Mom. I'll leave this morning. Ok. Yes. I'll be there by this afternoon."

David's heart dropped to his knees. What had happened to make Lexy leave today? Was it her dad or one of her brothers? No, it was something to do with Brody. Wasn't that the name of the guy she was dating? The fingers of jealousy started to grip his mind, but he shook them off; instead focusing on her facial expressions. Lexy ended the call and looked at him; David wrapped her in his embrace as her body shook with sobs. Whatever happened it was breaking her heart. She finally pulled back and stepped away. David resisted the urge to wipe away her tears. "It's Brody. He apparently had too much to drink at a party and got in a car accident. The person he hit was killed instantly. He is in intensive care with major injuries." David waited. "They're not sure if he will make it."

All feelings of jealousy faded away. Lexy had said they were more friends than anything. He couldn't imagine how he would feel if he got a phone call about someone close to him, or even Macy. It would be hard. "I'm sorry, honey."

Lexy reached out for his hand. He gave it to her. "I have to go." And as if an electrical current shocked her into action, she dropped his hand and took off running. David recognized her reaction as one of shock. He knew he couldn't let her go anywhere by herself. It took all of his stamina to sprint the mile and a half to keep up with her. When they reached the end of the trail, she didn't stop, but continued going towards the bridge and up the stairs.

He tried to catch his breath. "Lexy, wait." He knew his voice sounded harsh, it was his coaching voice, but he wanted her attention. He got it. She turned around to face him and David could see she was in no condition to make decisions. He also knew he was facing a stubborn streak he was all too familiar with. "Give me your keys."

To his surprise, she didn't put up a fight. She dug them out of the pocket of her shorts. He took her hand and walked her the rest of the way to the car. David opened the passenger side and physically sat her in the seat. He put her seatbelt on her and slid into the driver's side. He turned to her and took both her hands in his. "Let's pray."

She nodded.

"Father, we lift Brody up to you right now. We know he made a mistake, but we ask for mercy on His life. Please place your healing hands on him." David's voice cracked. "And be with Lexy, Father. Her heart is breaking and she needs strength to get back home. Help her know what to do and how to be there for Brody and his family. In your name. Amen."

Lexy opened her eyes and leaned her forehead on David's. "Thank you."

David knew the words were from the deepest place in her heart. He started the jeep and drove towards Jo's in silence. Lexy didn't let go of his hand except when he needed to shift the gears. Luckily, Jo had already received a phone call from Mrs. King and had all of Lexy's things packed by the time David pulled into the driveway. She met them in the driveway with her own bag packed. David let go of Lexy's hand long enough to get out of the jeep and whisper a few words to Jo. Lexy didn't move. Jo moved around to Lexy's side of the jeep. Lexy got out to let her in, but when her tennis shoe hit the ground she melted into

Jo's waiting arms. David's heart wrenched as he listened to her sob. Finally, after what seemed like days, Lexy composed herself. Jo decided to let David drive them back to The Locks to retrieve his car and then she would ride to Jacksonville with Lexy. She would take a plane back to Augusta.

David, reluctant to leave Lexy, but satisfied that she was in Jo's capable hands enveloped Lexy in a hug, whispering, "It's going to be ok."

She smiled a wobbly response, reached up and kissed him on the cheek.

Jo hugged him, patting his back. "I'll make sure she's ok, David." All he could do was nod and watch in quiet desperation as they drove away.

Lexy hadn't mumbled five words by the time they made the Florida line. She was thinking and praying. What would have made Brody drink? He never drank. Once in a while, she would see him hold a beer, but he nursed it and never drank more than one. And driving? He was adamant about drinking and driving. He was always the designated driver whenever any of his frat brothers went out. The whole thing didn't make sense. But the words from their last phone call rung in

Lexy's ears. She had just told Brody she thought they needed a break. He was silent for several seconds, before saying words that she would never forget. "I can't live without you, Lexy." Hearing those words then had infuriated her, because she saw them as a power play. She saw them as a way to keep her tied to him. But now, well what if….? She couldn't even finish the thought. Jo had been quiet the whole ride, not asking her questions, but just letting her process everything. She was grateful. Lexy could still feel David's hand in hers. She could still feel his kiss on the top of her hair. Her heart ached for his presence, and then guilt would consume her. She needed to be praying for Brody.

Finally, they reached the Jacksonville city limits and minutes later they were driving into a parking space at Memorial Hospital. Lexy had called her parents and they were going to meet her and Jo in the intensive care unit waiting area. Jo followed closely behind Lexy as they entered the hospital and found the elevator. Lexy could feel her stomach drop at the smells around her. They were smells of sickness and death. She almost lost whatever juice and crackers she had that morning when the beep of the elevator door and her father's face saved her from dissolving. She melted into her daddy's arms and he held her for what had to be five minutes. Lexy could sense her mother beside him but what she needed right now were the strong arms of her father. Finally she pulled away as he pushed the stray hairs back from her face. She hugged her mother and found the words, "How is he?" Jo hugged William and Elizabeth briefly as Lexy's dad led them down the hall to the waiting area. There she saw two of her friends from JU along with Brody's parents and his sister, Addie. Lexy went to all of them, hugging them, and saying she was sorry. They hugged her back but Lexy could tell they were trying to process the horrible situation. She crossed over to an empty chair beside her father, mother, and Jo. Finally, Lexy got the answer to the question she had asked.

Elizabeth reached over and took her daughter's hand. The look in her mom's eyes made her dread the answer. "He's awake, but…."

She looked over at her husband for strength. William knelt down in front of Lexy. There were tears in his eyes. "He has a spinal cord injury. He's paralyzed from the waist down, baby."

Lexy stood up immediately and walked down the hallway of the hospital, leaving the rest behind. Wide eyes followed her, but she didn't care. This couldn't be happening. Not Brody. He's an athlete, a golden boy; he's only twenty two. He's going to be an attorney. *God, where are You? Please, be with Brody. Please heal him. There has to be a way to make him better. Oh, God. It was only one mistake.* She could feel the hot tears coursing down her face. What about the person that was killed? What about that family?

Trust, Lexy...

Lexy held her head in her hands. She knew God's voice. Trust. But how? David was six hours away. Brody was lying in a hospital bed. Her world was falling apart. *Lean not on your own understanding....*

Again, the voice.

"Alexandra!"

Her father's tone made her turn around. William King reached out to her, and once again she fell in his arms, but this time there were no tears, just questions. "Daddy, what happened?"

"Honey, Brody's friends said he had been depressed lately."

Lexy felt like a boulder had landed in her stomach, and apparently her father sensed it. He took his chin in her hand and made her look at him.

"No m'am, Alexandra. This was not your fault. Brody made a bad decision, several of them, and the consequences were immediate and harsh. You will be his friend and comfort him as much as you can but you, under no circumstances, will feel responsible for this."

Lexy nodded, trying to believe her father's words. "Lexy…." The use of her nickname got her attention. "You can't take on the guilt from this; it will cripple you, in a way much worse than Brody. Do you understand?"

She did. She understood. Her father's words spoke to her head; however, they might take a little time to resonate in her heart. "Anyway, Brody was at a party. He had a few beers, but decided to leave before anyone else was ready. His friends tried to stop him, but he took off anyway." Her father stopped, trying to find the words for the next part. "He was on the interstate and crossed over the line. He sideswiped a car and it flipped. Brody's car hit some construction cross hares. The woman in the car was killed instantly. She was by herself."

Lexy swallowed. "Was she a…..?"

William nodded. "She was in her thirties, a mother of two."

Lexy closed her eyes and let the tears flow. "Daddy...."

"I know, baby. I know."

"Lexy?" This time the voice came from Addie, Brody's sister.

Lexy looked over her father's shoulder with raised eyebrows. Addie was only fifteen, but the last twenty four hours had obviously made her look much older; she was dealing with things no fifteen year old should have to think about. "Brody wants to see you, Lexy."

"Ok." Lexy pulled away from her dad, stepping towards Addie. Her father started to object, but Lexy shook her head. "I need to do this Daddy."

He looked at her for a long time and then both hands on her shoulders and looked her in the eyes. "Remember what I said?"

"Yes."

Lexy followed Addie into the ICU area. She caught her breath when she rounded the corner and saw Brody's blonde hair matted to his head. There was a sheet covering his legs; he wore a hospital gown, there was an IV. The last time she saw him he was standing. Would he ever stand again? He turned and looked at her, his blue eyes shining with sorrow, and she could feel her heart breaking. His voice was scratchy as he put his arms out towards her. She walked to him, gently embracing him. "You came."

She nodded her head. "Of course, Brody." She pulled back from him. "I'm so sorry this happened."

"Did they tell you about...." He looked down at his legs.

She smoothed the hair back from his forehead. "Yeah, they told me."

Giant tears rolled down his cheeks. "And the woman..."

She whispered, swallowing. "I know, Brody."

He shook his head. "I don't know what happened Lexy. I mean, it all started with one beer, then another, then soon I lost count. Things haven't been the same since you left. I knew I was losing you..."

"Brody..."

"No, let me finish. This isn't a guilt trip. I promise. But you need to know the truth. I was past drunk, Lexy. I don't even remember getting in the car. The only thing I remember is waking up with people working on me, and then the realization I couldn't feel my legs. They told me about everything else later."

Her eyes swept the length of his body. "I don't know what to say, Brody. I'll do anything I can to help."

Brody looked angry and she wasn't sure where his anger was directed. His words sounded forced. "You can't, Lexy. I'm paralyzed and have killed someone. I took a mother away from her children. I'm going to jail for a long time and I totally deserve it." His voice broke.

Lexy tried to reach out to him but he waved her off.

"God still loves me. I know all that, but He and I have some talking to do. He's all I have right now." He turned over and leveled her with his eyes. The words of her mother replayed in her head, '*when He is all you have, He is all you need...*' She looked at Brody as he begged his next words. "I need you to go away."

Lexy's heart stopped. That wasn't what she was expecting to hear. "Brody...I...I want to be your friend."

"But you can't, Lexy. Not now. I'm in love with you. I've been in love with you. And I know you're not in love with me. I've known it for a long time, and should have let you go a long time ago. One day, when I've got this all figured out, you can be my friend again. But for now, I need you to go. Promise me you'll go."

Lexy couldn't stop the sobs escaping from her throat. She laid her head on his chest.

"Brody, I don't want to go." She didn't miss the irony of the second time that day she had uttered those very words and the difference in circumstances. She could feel him stroking her hair, and then finally she really heard his plea. "Please, Lexy. Please leave."

She stood up and wiped her eyes. "Ok, Brody. I'll go. But remember this isn't the end. Please know that God has a purpose for you."

He nodded and whispered. "Go. Please send my parents in; I need to see them."

Lexy walked to the waiting room and asked Brody's parents to go to him. Lexy hugged them both as they walked toward their suffering son hand in hand. She looked at her own parents and Jo and motioned them toward her. "It's time to go. I'll explain later, but we need to leave." They didn't question her, but followed her to the parking lot. She explained as best she could. She wasn't sure if she understood Brody's request, but all she could do was honor it. Lexy looked from her dad to her mom, and finally to Jo. "I want to go home." William nodded and led them all to their vehicles. "Let's go, ladies."

Lexy woke up to voices downstairs. She blinked and focused her eyes on her surroundings. She was home. A feeling of warmth rose up as she snuggled deeper into the comforter that had done its job for the last ten years. But then she remembered why she was home and all the comforts in the world couldn't take away the dawning sadness in her heart. Brody. She immediately closed her eyes and began praying. *Lord, I so didn't expect this. He wants me to stay away. Is that what you want, Lord? I understand his reasoning, but I can't even be there as his friend?* Lexy blinked back fresh tears; it didn't seem fair. Then as He often did, the whisper of a verse came to Lexy's mind as an answer to her prayer. *Trust in the Lord with all your heart, lean not on your own understanding, in all your ways acknowledge him and he will make your paths straight.* Lexy closed her eyes and prayed through the verse asking God for strength and dignity. After ten minutes, Lexy threw back the covers, grabbed her robe and started down the stairs. When she got about half way down, the voices of Jo and her parents drifted up along with the smell of bacon and coffee. For some reason, Lexy decided to sit and listen, rather than join them.

"You should be very proud of your daughter, guys. She did a beautiful job directing that camp. The volunteers and the campers loved her." Jo's voice held great affection as she spoke.

"We had a feeling she would really love it." Lexy could picture her mother looking at her father knowingly as she said her next words. "Jo, what else happened with Lexy while she was up there?"

Several seconds passed before Jo answered. "What did Lexy tell you?"

This time Lexy's father spoke. "She told us a little about David, how he knew the boys in college, how he came to Christ. What kind of boy is he?"

Jo laughed. "Well Will, he's not a boy. He's a man with a career and a past. Not a sordid one, but he's not exactly wet behind the ears either."

William King cleared his throat. "I don't mind the past, Jo. But what kind of man is he now?"

"He's strong in his faith and he loves your daughter."

Lexy covered her mouth. *He loves me.* It wasn't that the words surprised her; in her heart she knew, and she felt the same way, but hearing them now; it made her want to wiggle her nose bewitched style and wrap herself in his embrace. Elizabeth's voice came in a whisper. "How do you know he loves her Jo?"

"He told me." Lexy's heart was now in her throat and it took everything she had not to scream when a hand appeared on her shoulder. She turned and saw Brad looking down at her. He motioned for her to follow him. When they reached the top of the stairs and out of earshot, she punched him in the arm. "You scared me to death." She then remembered she hadn't seen him in two months and literally jumped in his arms. He was laughing. "Hey, Sis."

"Hey."

"We missed you."

"You, too."

He held her back and looked at her a long time. "I'm sorry about Brody."

Lexy nodded. "Me too."

Brad led her to their media room that had served as a romper place for them through their teenage years. There were overstuffed denim covered chairs, bean bags, a big screened television with every video game imaginable, and a pool table. Her parents' philosophy was that they would rather their children and their friends hang out here than anywhere else, so they made it as welcoming as possible. Lexy had always been grateful.

She plopped down on one of the giant bean bags and leaned her head back.

"So, you met David Griffin, huh?"

Lexy's head popped up. "How did you know?"

"News travels, Lexy. You should know that."

Brad stared at her; Lexy really never noticed how much her identical brothers looked like her father, but Brad especially did when wearing the older King's cross examination expression.

"What?" She finally said.

"You love him, don't you."

Lexy rolled her eyes and covered her face with a pillow. She grunted in exasperation and threw the pillow at Brad.

"What was that for?"

Lexy stood up and began pacing the room. "I don't know. Yeah, I love him. But Brad, how is this supposed to work?"

Brad was smiling and it irritated her. "What are you smiling at?"

"You. My little sister's in love...." He sang it like a teasing third grader.

She threw him her best look of warning. "You're seriously going to get hurt."

He threw the pillow back at her. "I'll risk it. David's awesome, Lexy. Billy and I always wished we hadn't lost touch after college. I'm glad to know he's still walking in his faith."

Lexy fell back down on the bean bag. "He is. He's very strong. And proud. And aggravating. And overprotective. And caring. And he's a gentleman."

"And you're in love with him…"

She stopped and nodded her head slowly.

Brad shrugged his shoulders. "So what's the problem?"

Her eyes widened at her brother's obvious denseness. "Problem? Oh, I don't know, Brad. Five hours apart for starters. Then there is the little factor that he has a full blown career and I don't have one at all. I'm not even sure what I'm going to do with my life."

The teasing light in her brother's eyes had gone, and sympathy replaced it. "Still no decisions, huh?"

"No. I mean, yes. I want to teach."

"Then teach."

"It's not that simple, Brad."

"Oh really? Is there a sudden shortage in special education positions that I'm not aware of? Seriously, Lexy. You're making it harder than it is. Do like you've done since you could walk; jump in full force and give it a shot. If you don't like it, do something else."

205

Lexy looked at her brother and knew he was right, but he wasn't finished.

"The real problem you have is deciding where to do it. Do you move up to Augusta and begin a career and a relationship at the same time?" He shook his head. "That would be tough." Lexy looked at her brother and knew she couldn't do that; not right now.

"No, I have to walk before I can run, Brad. Believe me, everything in me wants to run to David. But I can't. I have to figure some things out on my own."

Brad stood up. "Well, sorry to have interrupted your morning of eavesdropping, but I have to admit it was fun. It's been years since I caught you on your favorite step."

Lexy rolled her eyes, but then got up to move towards her big brother. "Seriously, Brad. Thanks. Whatever happens, you'll never know how much of a support system you and Billy have been to me. I love you."

Brad ruffled her hair like he did when she was five. "Love you too, Lexy. Sara and I will be praying for you."

"Thanks, Brad."

The Jacksonville International Airport buzzed with activity. Lexy kept Jo at the gate where flight 115 would soon depart. She reluctantly let go when the final boarding call came over the loud speaker.

Jo looked at the younger woman with love in her eyes. "Are you sure you don't want to come back, even for a few days?"

She had thought about it, dreamt about seeing David again, but in her heart she knew now was not the right time. Going to Augusta would mean bringing a lot of baggage that needed to be checked at this point in her life. Once it was taken care of, she would go to him. She just prayed he was still there. Lexy shook her head, but handed Jo a sealed envelope marked David. "Please give this to him. It's the best I can do right now." She hugged Jo one more time. "Thanks for everything. Give Frannie a hug for me. I love you."

Jo turned and walked away and Lexy wiped her eyes as she watched her rush toward her flight. She took a deep breath and mentally told herself to pull herself up by the bootstraps as her grandmother used to say. She had some work to do, and there was no better time than the present.

Chapter 11
5 months later

Lexy took one final look at the classroom that had been her place of employment since August. It had been quite a ride, teaching high school students with behavior disorders and learning disabilities, but she had grown so much in the process, it was completely worth it. God moved quickly when she received that phone call to fill in for a local high school teacher going on maternity leave. But Lexy accepted the job immediately, knowing it was exactly what she needed. During her interim teaching, she learned so much about the system and content matter, along with specific disabilities. She worked with parents and other teachers, collaborated on committees, and in the end had received a permanent job offer beginning after Christmas break. And through it all she decided Tommy Griffin was the wisest high school student she had ever met. He was right; the kids needed people like her, not that she was a stellar instructor, but she had a calling and God confirmed it every single day she was in the classroom. Lexy gathered all of her things, took one final look around Room 216, and shut the door behind her. She thought about Brody. The husband of the wife and mother who was killed asked the judge for leniency; Brody got thirty years of probation and five years of community service. He was healing, and had even found someone to love him like he wanted to be loved. Suzie was a girl they had known in college, one that came to visit him while he was in rehab. Reports were they got engaged a week ago. Brody had made contact with Lexy in October, asking if he could come and talk to her students about drinking and driving. She agreed wholeheartedly, and through that speaking engagement she knew she and Brody had made progress. Shades of their friendship were evident now that Brody knew what true love was; she was so happy for him she could almost burst.

Lexy took a deep breath as she moved on to new things. The school that had been home away from home was in her rearview mirror, and Lexy knew now more than ever it had been a good experience, one she had needed. But now it was time to take care of some unfinished business. She had a date with a coach in Georgia.

"Coach Griffin!"

David looked at Michael, his quarterback and made the signal. It was a major chance, one that would make him the hero of the night if it worked, or one that might cost him his job if it failed. It was the state championship and the Hawks were trailing by one point. There were five seconds on the clock. He could go for the extra point, tie the game, and go into overtime or go for a two point conversion and win it right now. *God, I know you're with me. Even in the small stuff. These boys have worked hard and so have I; you've seen me through a lot this fall, starting with a broken heart. But this is you God. Regardless of the outcome, this is you.* And as the play started, David held his breath and watched in awe as his boys got the two points and won the game. The crowd behind him was on their feet and began to cheer wildly. They had won the state championship. David was swept up in hugs from the players and other coaches; he ducked anticipating the cooler of iced PowerAde as it soaked his apparel. He said a silent prayer of thanksgiving as he was swarmed by his mother, Tommy, Jo, Frannie, and many other people in the community. The adrenaline filled minutes when he talked to his players, and told them how proud he was of them helped fill the void in his heart, despite all the excitement. He missed her more than he could express in words; she

211

was the one person he wanted to hold right now. It was the biggest success of his career and he wanted to share it with who he believed was the love of his life. In her letter, she had asked for time and he gave it. He let her be. There were times he actually got in his truck and made it as far as the interstate before he turned around, knowing he couldn't ambush her; she had to figure some things out. He respected that; respected her. But, oh, how he longed to hold her for a few minutes.

After a shower and some time alone with God, David came out of the locker room and looked around the stadium; everyone except for a handful of people had cleared out. He sat on the bench and took inventory of himself. He had peace about Lexy, peace that one day they would be together. But how long was one day? Tommy had pulled him aside minutes after the win and looked at him with his grown up eyes. "It's time to go to her now, David." A vicious coughing fit interrupted his flow, but the message came across. "It's time." The winter months were tough on Tommy and he had been in the hospital more than out, but he made his mother bring him. David suspected his motives were more to talk to his idiot big brother, than actually watch the football game. But now that David was all alone and the background noise had faded, he knew it was time to see her. He thought of the duffel bag of extra clothes he kept in his truck and decided it might be wise to drive through the night. Walking across the field, he began formulating a plan of attack. He would drive to Jacksonville and find Brad; then he would go to her father's house. He would ask her father for permission to date her. He would do it the old fashioned way. David could close his eyes and see her face…--

"Ow! What in the…." David held his head and watched as a football rolled beside him. His heart was thumping out of his chest as he turned around, and his eyes focused on the only woman he ever truly loved. She was dressed in jeans, a bright pink sweater and striped scarf, a black pea coat and gloves. Her hair was tied back, but when she reached him he could see it was coming loose and falling around her flushed face. She wore a mischievous smile despite the wetness of her hazel eyes.

"Hi." It was the only word she could utter, but she was doing better than him because he had no words at all. He didn't care about appearances or that there were unanswered questions; all he cared about was that she was here. He scooped her up in one brief second and kissed her like there was no tomorrow. He could feel her gasp in surprise, but then delightfully return his affection with enthusiasm. David drew back, his senses in overload, and set her on the ground. The smile that lit up her face sent his heart reeling. "I love you, David." By this time, he couldn't stop the tears running down either of their faces. He shook his head, still not believing she was real. He held her face, caressing her wet cheeks. "Lexy, I..."

She reached up on her tip toes and silenced him with her finger. He took her gloved hand and held it up against his cheek, while she spoke. "I've missed you so much. Please know that every second I was away felt like forever, but God has used this time to fill in some gaps and answer some questions. But one that has been affirmed over and over is that, well...." She shook her head, trying to find the words. "I'm in love with you."

David bent down and touched his nose to hers. "Pup, I'm in love with you, too. I have been ever since you beat me in basketball."

She laughed and the frost lingered between them. David kissed her again and again and again. He whispered. "I have something to ask you. In fact, I was on my way. But I kind of need to talk to your dad first."

Lexy pulled back with a knowing smile, her eyes shining. "Do you now?"

"Yeah. Wanna drive to Jacksonville?"

She stepped an arm's length away and thought a second, then shook her head. "No."

David looked at her smile in confusion. "No? But…"

Her eyes were dancing. "I brought my dad with me, along with my mom and my brother and his wife. They had to help me move."

David knew his eyes looked like saucers, but he thought he misunderstood her. "Move?"

She put her hands on her hips in Lexy fashion. "Well, now I'm good, but not that good. I can't move everything I own by myself. I needed a little help. Especially since I start my new job at Central High School in two weeks."

David's mouth hung open as Lexy turned around and behind the bleachers he saw what had to be her family accompanied by a scheming Frannie and Jo, and even Tommy and his mother.

Lexy motioned to them to come over. "Do you want to have that talk right now or wait until we've had some dinner?"

David put his arm around her and kissed her once more. "I've waited long enough, Lexy. Right now would be good."

Epilogue

Her reflection dressed in a simple white gown, minutes away from becoming Mrs. David Griffin, was surreal to say the least. She wasn't nervous, although thoughts about the night to come gave her pet butterflies a reason to wake up and play; instead, she was a mixture of delight and wonder. She had dreamt of this day since she was old enough to comprehend what the white dress in the bridal magazine meant. She was a bride. The door cracked open and the sight of her mother's teary eyes meant it was almost time.

Her voice was barely above a whisper. "Lexy, you look like a princess."

"Thanks, Mama." She reached out to her mom and enveloped her in a hug. "And not just for the compliment; for everything. I have truly been blessed."

Her mom pulled back and smoothed out Lexy's veil. "Yes, you are blessed. But we have been too." Elizabeth took a deep breath. "Here." She handed Lexy a white envelope. "It's from your father." Lexy looked up with wide eyes. "He can't always say what he feels, especially when his baby is about to become a wife. Read it and know that the words are penned from your father's heart." Lexy could only nod as she watched her mother step out of the room. She sat down in a chair across from the mirror and shakily opened the letter. She pulled out one piece of stationary with King written in calligraphy on the top. Sure enough, the letter was in her father's handwriting.

Dear Alexandra,

As you know, your mother and I have prayed for you everyday during the last twenty three years of your life. We have prayed for you to fall in love with Jesus. We have prayed for you to realize your calling and follow it; we have prayed for your husband before we knew his name, and even now we are praying for what God has in store for you and David. But the moment you were born, the moment I laid eyes on you and realized that you were a gift from God in the form of a tiny baby, I had to say a special prayer, one that I think God lays on the heart of every father when they cast eyes on their baby girls; I had to give you back to God. You are my little girl; the light of my life, but you are God's daughter first. And I am so proud of you. Lexy, continue to grow in God's light, continue to love like you have been taught.

You will be an outstanding wife to David, as I am confidant he will be an outstanding husband to you. And you will always be my child. But remember above all else, you are the daughter of the one and only King of Kings.

Love always,
Daddy

Lexy finished, not even trying to keep the tears at bay. She always knew waterproof mascara was a brilliant invention. She said a silent prayer of thanksgiving for her wonderful father and his touching words. And like a gentle breeze, the words from Proverbs 31 danced across her eyes; she is clothed with strength and dignity; she can laugh at the days to come. Slowly, she stood up and looked in the mirror. Her hands moved over her white dress, her eyes narrowed in understanding as she laughed aloud, suppressing the urge to dance.

Soon, the door creaked and William King appeared. She walked into his open arms, noticing the tears on his cheek. He smelled of the cologne he had worn forever and his grip on her was one of goodbye. Thankfully, she looked up to see him smiling through his tears. He held her face tenderly. "I love you, baby girl."

"I love you, Daddy."

He put his arm out to escort her. "Shall we?"

She grabbed her bouquet and nodded her head. And as she walked down the aisle and held David's gaze in hers she thanked her father in heaven for the blessing of knowing He was there watching her—watching his daughter and smiling.